Mercury Raine: Ghost Broker

Other Series By

The Dread Penny Society

Storm Tide

Hope Springs

The Gents

The Lancaster Family

The Jonquil Brothers

The Huntresses

Savage Wells

Sarah's Sweet Treat Novellas

Mercury Raine: Ghost Broker

SARAH M. EDEN

Pineway
BOOKS

Copyright © 2025 by Sarah M. Eden

All rights reserved. No part of this publication may be reproduced, stored in a retrieval system, or transmitted in any form or by any means—electronic, mechanical, photocopying, recording, or otherwise—without the prior written permission of the publisher, except in the case of brief passages embodied in critical reviews and articles. This is a work of fiction. The characters, names, incidents, places, and dialogue are products of the author's imagination and are not to be construed as real.

ISBN: 978-1-968090-01-2

Cover design © Pineway Books

1

Mercury Raine had been born with neither rank nor wealth, but in a world in which ghosts were nearly as valuable, it wasn't truly a shock that he had made himself an inarguable success. He was the kingdom's most sought-after ghost broker, having facilitated countless specter swaps over the past decade.

Many did what he did, but none were as good at it as he.

Every year or so, Society decided it favored one type of ghost over another. Those with ghosts matching the current rage breathed a sigh of relief. Those without flocked to Mercury—hoping he had time for them and that they could afford his services.

He'd managed to toe the line of appearing to be wealthy and genteel enough to hail from Society while also adopting enough humility in his appearance to make his being in trade not so odd as it would be. And he had early on learned the importance of seeming to be older than he was without making him seem drastically beyond his actual thirty years. The balancing act was a precarious but necessary one. And he managed it, like everything else he did, brilliantly.

Lord Garston Peabody, younger son of the Duke of Fellington, had arrived two days earlier intent on trading his emotionally unstable ghost—out of fashion now—for a ghoul capable of lifting a particularly condescending eyebrow. Judgmental ghosts were all the rage in London. Among Mercury's ghoulish horde were four ghosts that Society would currently drool over, and the young lordling had narrowed his preference down to two.

Vernon the Vain and Testy Tolver, the subjects of Lord Garston's debate, were being very snooty about the whole thing, which was making his decision all the more difficult. And it didn't help that his current ghost repeatedly jumped between indifference over the entire thing and uncontrollable ghostly tears.

"I simply cannot choose," Lord Garston bemoaned, pacing the library for the second day in a row. "Society is so particular about these things. And it will be at least six months before I can trade again if I choose wrong. The Season will be over by then." His lordship knew the specifics because he came to Aventine Manor on a very regular basis looking to improve his spectral situation. The ghost he was trading out had, in fact, been traded *to* him only nine months earlier.

"Take your time." Mercury had grown quite adept at pretending to be patient.

His ghosts didn't usually bother.

As Mercury stepped from the library, leaving his indecisive customer to fret himself into a very lordly fit of nerves, he caught sight of several of his apparitions hovering in the corridor with their ghostly ears pressed to—and, in some cases, *into*—the walls, clearly listening in.

"He hasn't decided yet," Mercury told them.

"What's to decide?" Gary the Green tossed his translucent arms in the air. "Testy Tolver and Vernon the Vain are both miserable louts. Society would love either one."

"It's a shame the languishing lordling doesn't have more than one attachment. He could simply take them both." Mawky's hands were pressed to her heart—or where her heart would have been if she'd had a body—as she made the declaration, giving the impression of a martyr bravely walking to her doom.

"If Lord Garston had multiple attachments, he might decide to become a broker himself. We'd lose his business," Mercury reminded her. "He makes more frequent trades than anyone else in the entire kingdom. And he always brokers them here. His patronage is part of why we are so successful."

"And why we can be certain whichever obnoxious haunt he takes with him this time will be back within the year." Gary the Green sounded annoyed. He usually did.

Mercury passed through the gathered ghosts, *literally* in some cases. Experience told him that Lord Garston would require at least another day to make his decision. And, once a choice was made, it took another day for the switch to be made.

These things were both shockingly simple and impossibly complicated.

The number of ghosts attached to a person at birth was the number that person would always have: no more, no less. Most people's number was zero. Of those who had a ghostly attachment, nearly all could claim only one. But one was enough. The cachet of having a ghost was unsurpassed in Society. The better the ghost, the higher that person's standing rose.

A few people were born with more than one ghostly companion. Those with multiple ghosts had the ability to trade their ghosts for others', provided everyone ended those trades with the same number they began with.

Most brokers had three or four attachments to work with and lined their pockets quite nicely helping the socially ambitious obtain the most fashionable specters.

Three or four.

Mercury had twenty.

One of which was currently slamming a door down the corridor. Another floated across the window Mercury walked past. His more mischievous spirits liked to put on a show whenever someone came to negotiate an exchange. The chain-rattling in the north wing was a bit much, though.

He lowered himself into his favorite comfortable chair in his favorite comfortable sitting room. A ghostly hand offered him the latest copy of *The Times*—some ghosts could move objects in the physical world.

"I am pleased to report, Mr. Raine," this particular ghost—Smythe—said, "that there is still no indication Society is leaning toward a preference for butler ghosts."

"I suppose I'll be forced to keep you a bit longer." Mercury always made a show of being on the verge of trading away Smythe. Truth was, he never would. Smythe had been among his original twenty, and one of only three who were still with him.

Mercury unfolded the newspaper, skimming the headlines. The Prime Minister's ghost was proving a little *too* judgmental, leading to a great deal of consternation on the floor of the House of Commons.

"He should have brokered his exchange at Aventine Manor," Mercury muttered. The Prime Minister would have left with a ghost that could help his political *and* social prospects, and Mercury would have made a pretty penny for his efforts. They'd both lost out.

Baby Blue, a ghostly five-year-old boy in a blue tunic of centuries earlier, wandered in through the wall. He was one of Mercury's Originary ghosts, the term used for the ghosts a person was born with— one's *original* ghostly companions.

"I hope Lord Garston chooses Vernon the Vain," Baby Blue said.

"Why is that?" Mercury watched the tiny ghost over his newspaper.

"Because Testy Tolver is funnier. I think he should stay."

It was as good an argument as Mercury had heard. "But he does fit the current fashion. If Lord Garston doesn't pick him, the next person likely will."

Baby Blue plopped onto the floor, legs folded. He nodded toward the paper in Mercury's hands. "Are people wanting baby ghosts?"

"Wouldn't matter if they were," Mercury said. "I'm not trading you."

The little specter smiled, just as he always did when they had this discussion. Mercury teased Smythe about swapping him, but he'd learned very quickly not to take the same approach with Baby Blue.

Without warning, the air filled with a shrill and off-key operatic aria. "Blasted blazes," Mercury muttered.

He'd received Signora Bellona in a swap two years earlier, and he'd not been overly happy about it since. She fancied herself a performer, with all the world her stage. He suspected if ghosts could strangle each other, he'd have a not-so-mysterious murder to solve.

Six ghostly heads popped through the wall, all eyeing him accusatorially.

"How was I supposed to know this about her?" he demanded. "I'm a ghost broker; I don't have the second sight."

"Can't you trade her to someone?" Gary the Green demanded. "Judgmentalness *is* one of her Integral Traits."

"Our only hope is that she'll refrain from singing long enough for someone to take her," Captain Capitate grumbled.

"She managed it once before." Mercury's voice crackled with dry annoyance.

"Fooled us all." Mawky struck her constant post of hand-to-heart suffering as she floated through the walls. Martyrdom was one of her Integral Traits. "And how we suffer for it."

"I'll trade her if I can," Mercury assured them. "I know she wants to go back to the Continent, so that might encourage things."

Ghosts had some say in the brokering that occurred. If they were entirely opposed to a trade, it couldn't be made. But they were, almost without exception, very flexible and willing to change their connections. Mercury hadn't sorted out why that was.

Signora Bellona finished her unwanted performance. Out of habit, the ghosts all silently clapped. She demanded that when anyone was in the same room as she was when "blessing" everyone with her "talents." Baby Blue tossed himself onto the floor in a posture of absolute relief. Mawky ended her clapping and immediately pressed her hand dramatically to her ghostly heart once more.

Smythe returned to the room. He had to pass through Captain Capitate to do so. Ghosts weren't able to exceed five hundred feet away from the person they were attached to but could otherwise wander at will. Most of Mercury's ghosts liked staying close, which meant even large rooms could be a little crowded. Smaller ones, like this, were sometimes packed to the very rafters. "You are needed downstairs, Mr. Raine."

"Has Lord Garston made a decision?" Mercury hadn't expected one so quickly.

"No, sir. A new client has arrived interested in brokering a swap."

"Not a *returning* client?" That was always good news.

"New. And, from the looks of them, they have both the means of securing a good trade and a place on the rungs of Society that would make them anxious to secure a truly beneficial ghost."

That *was* interesting.

Mercury stood. He smoothed first his paisley waistcoat and then his curly hair, making certain both were as they should be. Then he glanced around at those of his twenty ghosts who were in the room. "A new client." He made sure they'd heard that bit. "You all know what to do."

2

Mercury tugged at the cuffs of what Baby Blue called his "business coat." It was the one he always wore when greeting a client upon arriving at Aventine Manor, whether that client was new or returning. The dark gray was a somber color that conveyed capability, but the cut and fit were fashionable and spoke of wealth and influence. Both were essential in his line of work.

He paused a moment at the top of the grand staircase. He knew he was visible from the client table below, where Smythe would have directed the new arrivals to wait. Tipping his top hat the tiniest bit askew, he began the slow and steady descent. Right on cue, his ghosts began floating across his path from all directions, one at a time, dramatic, impressive, and just a little theatrical. They swirled around, hovering lower and lower as he descended.

Mercury could now see the table where his newest potential clients sat. He felt certain they were a mother and daughter, clearly of the upper class, the younger of the ladies likely in her twenties. Hovering near them was an elderly ghost watching the swirling and floating with wide, translucent eyes.

But to which of the two ladies was the ghoul attached?

Utilizing a well-rehearsed wave of his arms, Mercury dismissed his ghostly companions. Their sudden flight had the usual effect: both ladies looked impressed. A good start.

He smoothly removed his hat, set it on the seat of an empty chair, and set his curls to rights once more before sitting on a different one, facing the ladies from across the tea-and-scones-spread table. "I'm Mercury Raine. What can I do for you?"

The assumed mother leaned eagerly toward him. "I'm Mrs. Huddleston. This is my daughter, Miss Huddleston."

He dipped his head to them in turn.

"We simply cannot go to London for the Season with such a non-judgmental ghost." Mrs. Huddleston motioned toward the elderly specter still standing wide-eyed behind the two ladies. "We are told by simply everyone that you are the premier ghost broker in all the kingdom."

"Flattery will get you everywhere, Mrs. Huddleston."

She smiled broadly. Her daughter appeared to be listening. What she did not appear to be was impressed.

"Who was your previous broker?" Mercury asked, not caring which of them answered.

"This is our first trade," Mrs. Huddleston said. "We aren't even entirely certain how the process works."

Mercury let his eyes dart to Miss Huddleston, doing an on-the-spot evaluation. He had become a quick study of people over the years. Generally, he could accurately ascertain connections and personalities within moments of meeting people. The mother in this duo was domineering. Her daughter looked almost bored but was clearly listening. Miss Huddleston had what seemed to be an intellectual curiosity about the matter, but Mrs. Huddleston had an eager passion for the undertaking.

The mother, then, was most likely the one to whom the elderly ghost was attached.

"Allow me to explain," he said with one of his winning smiles. "You cannot sell or simply unattach yourself to a ghost. You arrive with a ghost; you leave with a ghost. Whether or not it is the *same* ghost depends on a few things. The one with the attachment has to, in the end, choose to make the exchange. Neither ghost can be openly opposed to the swap."

"The *ghosts* get to choose?" Mrs. Huddleston sounded horrified.

The silent Miss Huddleston's expression changed for the first time. She shifted from almost indifferent to disapproving, though he thought she might have been reacting to her mother rather than to the idea of ghosts *not* being forced into transfers.

"They don't get to choose in the same way their human counterparts do," Mercury clarified, "but neither can they be exchanged if they are firmly opposed to the trade. Also, a first trade is a more complicated one."

"In what way?" Mrs. Huddleston didn't seem pleased by the idea of complicated.

"It cannot be completed if any immediate family members in the same household are opposed to it. A person's first ghost is likely to have been part of that household for years. The prevailing theory is that the trading of a ghost so connected to a household impacts that household, and thus there cannot be vehement objections."

Mrs. Huddleston watched him closely, nodding along with his explanation. Her daughter simply watched him.

"Are there any other members of your family in your household?" Mercury asked.

"No," Mrs. Huddleston said. "Only the two of us."

That would simplify things.

"The Season will be in full swing in only another fortnight." Mrs. Huddleston's already clasped hands turned white-knuckled. "How long is this process likely to take?"

"That depends on how long it takes for a ghost to be chosen for the swap," Mercury said.

"How many ghosts do you have?" Mrs. Huddleston asked.

"A lot."

"The rumor is you have a dozen."

Mercury only nodded. Even his ghosts themselves didn't know his actual number. Society was astounded at the possibility of twelve. But he had nearly twice that many.

"And after a ghost has been chosen?" Mrs. Huddleston asked. "What happens then?"

Miss Huddleston sat in silence, seemingly neither impressed nor interested in being part of the conversation. Interesting.

"Once the ghosts decree that they are not opposed to the trade," Mercury continued, "then it can be accomplished within a few hours, usually."

Mrs. Huddleston released a slow, dignified, relieved breath. "Then we still have time. We simply cannot arrive in Town with an unfashionable ghost. We cannot." She gave a firm nod. "We would like to ask you to broker this ghost exchange."

That was easy enough.

Mercury stood and took up his hat once more, though he didn't put it on his head yet. "Your traveling trunks will be placed in guest chambers." One of the benefits of having a ghost butler with the ability to move physical items. "Explore the estate at your leisure. You will most certainly encounter the ghosts. Get to know them as you are able. I will see you both again at dinner."

He dipped a quick bow to first the mother and then the daughter before setting his hat on his head and turning about. He undertook his usual polished and confident exit, knowing it left his clients with the assurance that they had come to exactly the right place for all their ghostly business.

Mercury had, for a decade, been the foremost ghost broker in all of the kingdom for a reason: he was remarkably good at every part of what he did.

3

Aventine Manor was never truly quiet. Mercury had learned as a child that having twenty ghostly attachments meant no space he occupied ever came close to silent. He didn't mind.

Mercury had grown up in an overcrowded, understaffed orphanage. He'd never been alone for reasons that had nothing to do with ghosts. Yet, he'd been lonely. His ghosts had mingled with those attached to other orphans in the facility. The orphanage governor had known Mercury possessed multiple attachments but had never been able to pin down precisely how many. That, in the end, had been both a saving grace and a means of escape.

Orphans with ghosts were adopted more readily than those without. They could provide additional cachet to any family who took them in. An orphan with multiple attachments ought to have been snatched up the moment he'd been left on the doorstep. But Mercury's most troublesome ghosts had been the ones who kept near at hand, making would-be adopters nervous. And when the governor had been forced to admit that he didn't know which of the remaining ghosts would become part of the potential family's household, every single interested party had quickly decided against taking the risk.

Saving grace and escape, indeed.

There was still no one, person or ghost, who knew how many attachments he had. Mercury had learned at a very young age that ghosts could keep themselves a secret even from each other. Avoiding interactions or not acknowledging to whom they were attached granted them some anonymity. Mercury himself hadn't known until he'd left the orphanage precisely how many or which of the ghosts there were his. There had been no one there to explain to him how to make sense of it.

No one knew he was the boy who'd run from the orphanage at thirteen years old. No one knew he'd circumvented the very strict laws about orphans trading ghosts. No one knew how quickly everything he'd built could be taken away from him.

He thought on that as he pondered the Huddlestons and which of his ghosts they might, in the end, choose. Every new client both solidified his success and left him keenly aware of how precarious it was under the surface.

Mercury had gone over his ledgers and taken a leisurely stroll about the grounds of his grand home by the time he returned to the house to dress for dinner.

He liked to give clients, new and returning, a feeling of freedom at Aventine Manor. He'd found early on in his work as a broker that even those who didn't feel any sort of connection to their ghostly attachments still found the process of swapping that ghost unexpectedly personal. If he stood nearby while they interacted and discussed their impressions, then they were less likely to make a decision and far less likely to feel confident enough in that decision for the transfer to take.

The Huddleston ladies should have had ample time to feel at home and even meet a few of the ghosts. Still, he meant to keep his distance until dinner.

His path down one of the corridors took him past Vernon the Vain and Testy Tolver. Neither was looking at the other, nor speaking, but it was obvious they were incredibly aware of each other and that they weren't overly pleased by that awareness.

"Has Lord Garston made a decision?" he asked them.

"Never met a more indecisive gentleman," Testy Tolver drawled, his wispy lip twitching in contempt.

"I don't know how he manages to feed himself with such an embarrassing inability to make choices." Vernon the Vain opted for a highly arched eyebrow.

Both ghosts likely realized how very difficult they were rendering Lord Garston's decision. He needed a judgmental ghost if he were to be at all fashionable this Season. These two took judgmental to entirely new levels.

Mercury had taken quite a gamble in acquiring them the year before, counting on his hunch that their Integral Traits would be all the rage this year. He'd been correct about that; he usually was.

"I'm certain you've heard," Mercury said, "that we have newly arrived clients, also looking for a fashionable ghost for the Season. They may very well make a decision before he does."

"Untitled clients," Vernon the Vain said, switching which of his eyebrows was raised in disapproval. "They do seem to have money, though."

"Money does not buy rank," Testy Tolver declared. "And when it does, it hardly counts."

At that, they both floated away, the very picture of judgment and disapproval.

He didn't mind them, but he wasn't going to overly miss them when they were traded away.

He continued on his way, his path taking him past one of the large doors leading into the library. It was open, and he could see and hear what was occurring.

Mrs. Huddleston and her daughter were seated near the fireplace. Near them were Gary the Green and Weeping William, another of the resident ghosts whose moniker was incredibly fitting.

"It's little wonder you were traded," Mrs. Huddleston said to William. "Emotional ghosts are not really sought after this year."

"I didn't overly like the household I was in anyway," William said, sniffling, which was what he always did. "No doubt emotions will be in vogue again soon enough."

"Perhaps." Mrs. Huddleston's gaze shifted to Gary the Green. "How long have you been here? Were you recently traded? Have you been trying to get traded for some time?"

"I've been here just as long as I'd like to be and will continue to stay for as long as I choose. Unless, of course, an intriguing opportunity presents itself."

Many of the ghosts spoke of trades and swaps this way: interesting, intriguing, a chance to explore and see and do. And the vast majority of them didn't seem at all bothered by the constant trading. Mercury had worried about that a lot as he was growing up. He'd realized, even at a young age, that there were some ghosts who didn't want to be uprooted. And while they couldn't be transferred *entirely* against their will, there likely had been some who'd agreed to trades they didn't actually want.

As if thoughts of the past and those early years of uncertainty had summoned her, Twisty Zizzy swooped up next to him. Her worried gaze settled on the group at the fire inside the library. Zizzy was one of his Originary ghosts, one of the three remaining who'd been with him from the very beginning.

"Are these ladies kind?" Zizzy asked.

"I don't know yet."

"Are they rapid traders?"

"I don't think *they* know yet."

Rapid traders were those who switched out ghosts at the minimum six-month intervals, constantly changing and swapping. He glanced at Zizzy, knowing what he'd see but wanting to make certain he wasn't mistaken. As predicted, she looked worried. It was one of her Integral Traits.

He'd realized very early on, long before he had even contemplated being a broker, that Zizzy did not care for the idea of being traded. She was, in fact, a little terrified of it.

"I promised you that I would never swap you."

"I know." She didn't sound reassured; she seldom did.

"How long have I made this my business?" Mercury asked.

"Twelve years." Her response had the tone of an oft-repeated answer, and for good reason. They had this conversation on a shockingly regular basis.

"When I am acting as broker, ghosts have more than a mere voice in the matter; their wishes are always honored."

"But if someone offered you a great deal of money or a ghost you really wanted—"

"Even if I found myself a penniless pauper living on the streets of London, trailed by an entourage of poverty-stricken ghosts that no one wanted to trade for, one of those ghosts would always be you. Until the day you tell me otherwise in tones of eager excitement, you will always be with me."

"I couldn't imagine wanting to be with anyone else," she said with a firm nod.

"And I would miss you if you left," he said. "I can't say that about most of the ghosts who've been part of this horde."

That brought a fond smile to her face. Zizzy was young, likely in her early teens, and sweet-natured. Even when he had been younger than that, she'd felt like a little sister. He'd always been extraordinarily protective of her. Ghosts didn't age, so in reality, she had existed longer than fourteen years. But the characteristics of the age they appeared to be filled the depths of who they were. She would always be this uncertain child, afraid of being abandoned and forgotten. And he would spend all the time necessary making certain she knew that wasn't going to happen.

"Oh, dear," Zizzy said, her attention in the library once more.

Mercury's eyes shifted in that direction too. Signora Bellona had just entered through the opposite wall as The Quiet Queen. Those two ghosts did not always get along. Only by threatening each of them with an underhanded swap that they would agree to and then regret—something he would never actually do, though he felt certain they didn't know that—had he negotiated something of a ceasefire between them. Heaven help him if everything came to a loggerhead now.

Mrs. Huddleston rose, her mouth dropping into an amazed O. Her head turned from side to side, looking first at one newly arrived ghost, then at the other, then back again.

The Quiet Queen was unmistakably judgmental. Mercury had no doubt he would gain quite a bit of money brokering her swap this Season. And she was anxious to go, so her cooperation was all but guaranteed. But until he saw the way Signora Bellona quickly evaluated Mrs. Huddleston, he'd not realized how judgmental she came across.

Very interesting.

"Oh, now we are getting somewhere," Mrs. Huddleston exclaimed.

The Quiet Queen and Signora Bellona both wrinkled their noses and twisted their mouths, nearly identical looks of disapproval. This might prove the fastest decision and transfer Mercury had ever brokered. It would be a helpful thing, as first swaps were usually the most time-consuming.

Mrs. Huddleston's ghost hovered in a corner of the room, watching the whole thing with a look that, once again, could only be described as overwhelmed.

Miss Huddleston proved most surprising of all. She was not watching her mother or the two ghosts who had captured her mother's attention. Neither did she seem overly interested in Gary the Green or Weeping William.

Her gaze was on *Mercury*.

4

Lord Garston's current ghost, Pearl, and Mrs. Huddleston's ghost, for whom Mercury did not yet have a name, hovered around the dining room during dinner. The room was large, though, capable of holding many more clients, their ghosts, and a number of Mercury's. Thus, dinner didn't feel crowded.

What it did feel was awkward.

Mrs. Huddleston had been excited to learn that the Duke of Fellington's younger son was at Aventine Manor. She hadn't stopped regaling the young lord with lists of people she knew that she was certain he did, and gatherings they had both been present at during the previous Season. Lord Garston was all politeness as he listened and all eagerness when he took over the conversation to offer up the same lists of his own.

If he'd chosen to, Mercury could have claimed a place in Society, one nearly rivaling that of a lord on account of his many ghosts. Even if he'd been willing to take the risk that such a public life would pose, if the interaction between Lord Garston and Mrs. Huddleston was what he'd have to look forward to, he had no intention of ever going to London.

He watched Pearl for a drawn-out moment, finding it odd that she was remaining in such close proximity to her current human attachment. She had resided at Aventine Manor for a couple of years before being traded to Lord Garston the year before. She knew that Mercury was not one of those hosts who felt uncomfortable with ghostly guests wandering about and making themselves at home. And while he found Lord Garston a little obnoxious and exhausting in all the wrong ways, Mercury knew him well enough to know that he wasn't one who grew difficult if his ghostly companion went too far afield. Why, then, was she staying at his side?

Her ghostly eyes flickered a couple of times to the elderly ghost wafting near the wall behind the Huddleston ladies. If he wasn't mistaken, there was outreach in her expression, as if she were hoping to offer her older counterpart a bit of reassurance and friendliness.

Of Mrs. Huddleston, Mercury asked, "Did you and your daughter go to London for the Season last year?"

Mrs. Huddleston's brow pulled tight. "Of course we did. That is what Lord Garston and I have been speaking of these fifteen minutes or more."

Mercury nodded. "I wasn't certain if all of those occasions were part of only the last Season or if you were speaking of enjoyable evenings spread out over several years." Truth be told, he hadn't been listening that closely. Still, it didn't do to admit to a client that she had the ability to drone on in such a way and on such mundane topics that a person feared for his continued mental stability were he to listen too closely.

Mrs. Huddleston launched very quickly into a discussion of the Duke and Duchess of Fellington's apparently very popular ball the year before. Lord Garston puffed up, quite pleased with the praise. Mercury would have had to work quite hard to care even less than he did about the topic.

He'd asked his question for entirely different reasons. He'd wanted to discover if Pearl and this elderly ghost had both been in London at the same time and present at some of the same gatherings. They had been. Pearl, then, was familiar with this new arrival, and she felt that the older specter needed a bit of looking after. That was exceptionally helpful information.

Mercury offered the still-unnamed ghost a friendly smile. "How did you enjoy London?" he asked her.

Her constant look of consternation shifted into something far closer to panic, which he hadn't been expecting.

Even more unexpected was that Miss Huddleston, who had literally not said a single word in the hours she and her mother had been at Aventine Manor, was the one who answered. "Timidity is one of Granny Grey's Integral Traits. Please do not require her to speak."

In quick and kind of frantic words, Mrs. Huddleston said to Lord Garston, "My daughter is merely overwhelmed. I assure you, she's not usually so forward. This is her very first transfer, and there's so much to think about and so much to do."

Miss Huddleston didn't argue or defend herself.

In a flash, the family's puzzle fell into place. Granny Grey, which was apparently this specter's name, was not *Mrs.* Huddleston's ghostly companion, but *Miss* Huddleston's. She was, as he suspected, something of a fragile ghoul, in need of care. And Miss Huddleston was protective of her.

He'd not known what to think of the younger of the two ladies. Her silence and her tendency to make certain she knew where Mercury was at any given moment had left him suspicious of her. The bigger issue was that *she* appeared to be suspicious of *him*.

Lord Garston turned an almost pitying look on Miss Huddleston. "I'm quite the expert in transfers, I assure you. I've undertaken at least a dozen trades. I would be happy to answer any questions you have or help you navigate it." Underlying that pity was, if Mercury wasn't mistaken, and he very seldom was, interest. Perhaps Lord Garston was hoping to leave Aventine Manor with more than just a ghost.

"Have you decided which ghost you intend to swap for, then?" he asked the young lord.

Pearl looked undeniably hopeful. Mercury didn't dare toss her the smile he felt. It was best not to tip one's hand. He would very much like having Pearl back for a time. She was a nice addition to the group, but he'd found that rapid traders like Lord Garston needed to feel they were coming out with the upper hand every time.

"I don't care to be rushed," Lord Garston said. "I have narrowed my list to two, but I might need a bit more time to decide which is ideal." His eyes darted to Miss Huddleston, though he likely thought he had hidden the movement. Mercury didn't miss much.

"I hope the two that you are considering aren't The Quiet Queen or Signora Bellona," Mrs. Huddleston said. "Those are the two that *we* have our eye on."

Lord Garston shook his head, the movement somehow both regal and a little pathetic. "Vernon the Vain and Testy Tolver. I think we will make an excellent pair, whichever I choose. I simply have to decide." He punctuated his declaration with a shrug that was no doubt meant to convey to all of them how commonplace such a difficult decision was for him, given his vast trading experience.

"Tell us about the Queen and the Signora," Mrs. Huddleston requested of Mercury.

"Both are very fond of social gatherings," he said, knowing that would appeal to a woman who was trading a ghost specifically for the purpose of parading it about in London. "Both are eager for trades, enjoy changes of scenery and companionship. So you are unlikely to have objections from either."

Mrs. Huddleston nodded eagerly, seemingly warming to her choices.

"And, as they have never shown any opposition to rapid trades," Mercury added, "you could broker another exchange as fashions change."

"Oh, excellent." Mrs. Huddleston clasped her hands together in excitement.

"How often are exchanges generally made?" Miss Huddleston asked.

Mercury couldn't tell if she was horrified, concerned, or merely curious. He was an excellent judge of character and could generally take a person's measure almost immediately. But she was eluding him.

"Six months has to pass before a new trade can be brokered," Lord Garston answered, jumping into the conversation with a beaming smile and a look of poorly disguised pride.

"If, Mr. Raine, you were to trade all of your ghosts within a few days of each other, then you could do no more trades for six more months?" she asked. "That must make being a successful ghost broker a little complicated."

He couldn't say anyone had ever sorted out that potential difficulty. Most didn't even think about it. Trading ghosts wasn't, in the minds of upper Society, much different from obtaining a new suit of clothing or a pair of matched horses. So long as they had what they wanted in the end, the work required to manage it was beneath their notice and thus of little concern.

"Those with multiple attachments are not limited in the frequency of their trades," Mercury explained. "Only those with a single attachment are time-limited."

She gave a ponderous nod, making him think hers was a genuine desire to understand better how the system worked.

Perhaps, as they moved forward, that could be a point of conversation, an opportunity for him to sort her out a little better. If she was to be a repeat client—and he always hoped people returned—it would help if he understood her preferences and character and which ghosts she was most likely to be happy with. In the end, he couldn't make the decision for his clients or his ghosts, but a good broker knew how to point both parties in the right direction.

"You have not addressed the most pressing matter," Mrs. Huddleston said.

"And what is that?" Mercury had long ago learned the trick of always being calm, no matter the aggravation.

"The Queen and the Signora are social and welcoming of change, travel, and new people. But will they judge people as harshly as current fashion demands?"

Mercury allowed a smile to spread slowly over his face. "I assure you, they are capable of mercilessly doing so."

That seemed to perk up Lord Garston. "Are they really?"

Mrs. Huddleston flashed an alarmed look at the gentleman she had only just been eager to impress. That gentleman looked suddenly even more indecisive than usual.

Miss Huddleston allowed the tiniest twitch of amusement.

The next few days could be interesting indeed.

5

Mercury awoke to the familiar sensation of being watched. He wasn't unnerved—a lifetime surrounded by ghosts had cured him of any tendency he might have had to react that way—but he *was* tired. He rubbed at his forehead. The room would be dark, but ghosts didn't have to be lit to be seen.

With a sigh, he forced his eyes open. It wasn't one of his ghosts hovering at the foot of his bed.

"Granny Grey." He blinked a few times, lingering sleep making his eyelids heavy. "Is something the matter?"

"You're Mercury Raine."

"I am."

"But you haven't always been."

Every bit of sleepiness fled in an instant. He'd hidden his identity quite well when beginning his brokerage. No one had, in twelve years, guessed that the name he had been using at eighteen years of age was not the one he'd been raised with. And he'd wager none of them would guess that his previous name had been given to him in an orphanage.

Mercury sat up, every instinct on alert. He was an orphan, and there were laws about orphans transferring ghosts. The orphanage that raised him had a claim on them all. He owed them for every Originary swap he'd made, and they could argue that every subsequent one was part of the debt. Running away from the orphanage, changing his name to hide his identity, and cutting them out of his subsequent business had been necessary for survival, but the law didn't particularly care about the well-being of orphans.

He was living a lie in many ways, and that was dangerous.

How much did Granny Grey know? He studied her, but his scrutiny made her very obviously and very sincerely nervous.

"You aren't afraid of me, are you?" he asked.

"I'm always a little afraid of everyone." Her ghostly voice shook a bit. "My Integral Trait."

"One of them," he countered. "I've yet to meet a ghost who doesn't have several."

That seemed to surprise her. Did she not know that she was more than that one characteristic?

"Mrs. Huddleston has said a few times that they've never undertaken a swap before." Mercury swung his legs over the side of the bed. "So, you're Miss Huddleston's Originary."

Granny Grey nodded, watching him warily.

"I promise you have no reason to be fearful of me."

"I can't help but be fearful." That was likely true. Integral Traits could not be changed nor minimized in a ghost.

He slid his feet into his slippers as he stood. Hoping to put her as much at ease as was possible for a ghost whose defining trait was never being at ease, he motioned slowly and gently toward the two chairs near the empty fireplace.

She floated in that direction and sat, to the extent a ghost could, in one of the chairs.

He sat in the other. "I realize this is an uncouth question, but it does help me broker swaps that are most likely to be pleasing to all involved... How old is Miss Huddleston?"

"Twenty-five."

"And has she done a great deal of traveling?"

"Only to London for the Season, and only the past five Seasons at that."

Granny Grey had likely not left the Huddlestons' country estate until five years earlier, long after Mercury had assumed his new name and buried his old identity. As far as he knew, no one in London had the first idea who he was. His Originaries would not be whispering about him, as that would put them in danger as well. So how did Granny Grey know that he wasn't who he said he was?

The question was a pressing one, yet the broker in him momentarily proved louder than the runaway orphan.

"Do you like Miss Huddleston?" he asked Granny Grey.

"She's lovely, and she looks out for me."

Interesting. When a person's Originary was an older one, usually it was the ghost who felt protective of their person.

"What about *Mrs.* Huddleston? Are you fond of her as well?"

Granny Grey didn't answer. Not at all. Which was an answer in and of itself.

"Have you had a chance since arriving at Aventine Manor to meet the ghosts here?"

"I am not... not overly skilled at... at conversations." In addition to worry, bashfulness seemed to be an Integral Trait of hers.

"I got the impression during dinner that you and Pearl are acquainted," he said.

"We met in London last Season."

Mercury smiled at her. "Pearl was one of the Aventine ghosts before she swapped to Lord Garston last year. We're excited at the possibility of her returning for a time."

"If Miss Huddleston trades me, how long would I stay here before I was swapped elsewhere?"

"That would depend a great deal on you," he said. "Some brokers are very concerned with the swiftest overturn they can manage. I prefer calm and comfort to efficiency, which means waiting until a ghost is more than merely *willing* to swap but *excited* to do so."

"You don't coerce anyone?"

"Ghost or person," he confirmed.

"I believe you, Mercury."

Her repeat of his name pushed all of his thoughts back to her declaration when he'd first awoken. "You know about me before I became Mercury Raine?"

She nodded.

"How long before?" He, after all, did not know his entire story, and learning it would be very helpful. Orphans who knew their parentage could be freed from the tie to their orphanage. All obligations to the horrid governor of that institution would be severed.

"Long enough." A cryptic and not overly helpful answer.

"Does Miss Huddleston know what you know about me?"

She shook her head.

"Does *Mrs.* Huddleston?"

Another shake of her translucent head.

"Then how do you?"

Her only answer was a smile, though not a threatening or sinister one. She stood, her feet a few inches off the ground.

"You won't tell me what you know or how?"

"I would like to stay at Aventine Manor," she said. "I will tell you once this is my home."

He stood as well. "I will do what I can."

She floated back toward the wall but stopped before passing through it. She turned back toward him. "There are others who know bits and pieces of you."

"Other ghosts?"

Granny Grey nodded. "And they are looking for you."

6

Mercury never fell back asleep. There were ghosts who knew something about who he was, and he didn't know the full extent of what that meant. If they knew only that he was an orphan who'd run out on his obligation, they could sink him. If they knew who he actually was, something *he* didn't know, they could save him.

He had to proceed with caution. Fortunately, he also knew to proceed with patience.

Lord Garston had seemed, as recently as the morning before, to be within a few hours of making his ghostly decision. Suddenly, he was entirely indecisive. Whether that was the result of Mrs. Huddleston pointing out the judgmental nature of The Quiet Queen and Signora Bellona, or the fact that Miss Huddleston was pretty and her mother clearly interested in making them a match, Mercury couldn't say. Regardless of the reason, Mercury had little choice but to wait.

He hadn't enough history with the Huddlestons to know quite how to proceed with them, which meant proceeding with cautious enthusiasm.

He arranged for a very pleasant game of lawn billiards the next day. It was a tactic he had often used. The grounds were beautiful and pleasant.

The back lawn offered a lovely view of both this estate and Larissa Lodge, a quaint house that had once served as the dower house for Aventine Manor. The environs helped people feel very pleased with their decision to seek out his brokerage services. And using those gorgeous grounds for a lighthearted diversion was doubly helpful.

One could learn a lot by watching a person play a game of little importance or skill. Most grow a bit less inhibited, relaxing and focusing on the bit of fun. They tended to reveal more of who they were because their guard was down.

Maybe when these unidentified ghosts who were looking for him finally found him, he ought to wrangle them into a very ghostly game of lawn billiards. Some ghosts could manipulate physical items, so there was even a chance the game could be played. He wanted to believe such an easy solution would work, but instinct told him the matter would be far more complicated.

"Excellently well played, Lord Garston," Mrs. Huddleston said after the young lord made a rather pathetic tap of the ball in the general direction he ought to have. Lord Garston puffed up immediately.

"I don't know which is more embarrassing," Vernon the Vain drawled, "her toadying or his lack of self-awareness."

Mercury quickly eyed the subjects of Vernon's evaluation. It was an insult, so they might very well feel offended. But it was also a moment of biting judgment, which was precisely what they both were looking for.

Lord Garston didn't seem to quite know how to respond. Mrs. Huddleston saved him the trouble.

"I can see why it is you are considering that particular swap," she said with enthusiasm. "How delightfully judgmental he is."

Lord Garston tipped his chin high and thrust his chest out. "I do have excellent judgment when it comes to ghosts."

If only Lord Garston knew how much the success of his repeated ghostly trades was owed to the fact that Mercury worked very hard to point him in the direction of choices that would work out well for all involved. Still, he had taken Lord Garston's measure long ago and knew the man was far more likely to be cooperative and pleased when he thought he was the resident genius.

Mrs. Huddleston whacked her mallet against a ball, sending it much closer to the target than her lordly co-competitor. To his credit, Lord Garston applauded and cheered her despite her ability laying bare how poorly his hit was.

"What an utterly tedious game." Signora Bellona sniffed loudly. "What would be far better—"

"No arias," Mercury said firmly, pointing at her in warning. The Huddlestons hadn't yet had enough time to decide if she was to their liking, and an impromptu off-key performance might put them off before they became enamored enough of her dismissiveness to be willing to endure her "talents."

The Signora's nostrils flared in absolutely unmistakable judginess. And that caught Mrs. Huddleston's attention.

Weeping William used his ghostly arms to rather expertly take his turn, he being one of those ghosts with the ability to move objects. Testy Tolver evaluated William's efforts with one muttered word of evaluation. "Acceptable."

That set William to weeping, which would have happened regardless.

Through it all, Miss Huddleston continued to prove an enigma. She didn't seem to not enjoy herself, but she wasn't openly enamored with the undertaking. While she clearly found it intriguing that his ghosts could manipulate physical things—something he didn't think Granny Grey could do—she wasn't overawed by it. She didn't show herself to be competitive nor upset if a turn did not go her way, but neither did she engage in a great deal of cheering and excitement on behalf of others who were participating.

What he had yet to discover was whether she was usually so unreadable or if she was hiding her true self. And if she was, why?

Still, the fact that she wasn't immediately pulled into the competition told him she was unlikely to be one whose quest for the latest and most fashionable of ghosts would lead to problematic frustration if her choice didn't prove as beneficial as she hoped. That took some of the pressure off. It also meant that she likely would make a pleasant companion for whichever ghost was chosen, even if that companionship did not last beyond the minimum six months. That also set his mind at ease.

He had swapped ghosts to people who were likely to be grumbly or snippy or even unkind. But he only ever did so if the ghosts in question understood the situation they were getting themselves into, would not be made entirely miserable by it, and were absolutely in favor of the switch. Even then, he always worried a little.

He didn't fully understand how much ghosts felt or how they experienced their version of the world. He didn't know if their emotions were the same as people's or if their feelings functioned similarly. All he had to go by was his very human version of life. He'd chosen to treat them as if they were identical, deciding that was a better approach than dismissing entirely the possibility that they could be made miserable and not doing anything to avoid it.

They are looking for you. Heaven help him if the ghosts Granny Grey spoke of cared little about his potential misery. They knew things, and he had to discover what. If she stayed at Aventine Manor, he would have time enough to begin piecing together that mystery. And if the Huddlestons made a transfer, Granny would be staying.

He simply had to facilitate that.

Mercury wandered a bit and stood beside Lord Garston. "I must add my compliments to those Mrs. Huddleston has already offered," Mercury said. "The two ghosts you are debating between are, without question, more than judgmental enough to be quite fashionable this Season. More than that, though, I can say they'll be a good fit for you. Not because they are judgmental, mind you. I am not attempting to cast such aspersions."

Lord Garston smiled, a sincere expression of understanding. They'd worked together quite often and, if nothing else, the young lord knew Mercury was not inclined to insult people.

"Neither would seem out of place at any of your family's most prestigious gatherings. It's well-spotted of you." Mercury knew to leave it at that.

Lord Garston was best approached in spurts. He would offer a little compliment or a little nudge in one direction or another, and then slip away while his lordship pondered what Mercury had said.

As he stepped away this time, his path took him near Miss Huddleston. They'd not exchanged more than five words since she and her mother had arrived the day before. Yet, he somehow felt they had interacted a great deal. Perhaps it was because he was constantly studying her. Perhaps it was because nearly every time he looked in her direction, she was looking in his.

"Have you had a chance to meet our ghosts?" Mercury asked.

"Quite a few," she said. "Though I don't know how many you actually have."

He didn't answer the implied question.

She didn't imply it again.

"I met Pearl in London," she said. "I understand she resided at Aventine Manor before transferring to Lord Garston."

"That's true."

"Do you see any of the ghosts again after they have swapped to someone else?" she asked.

"Only if they return with their current attachment, whoever that might be."

"Do you ever leave Aventine Manor?"

He shook his head. "I've not had any desire to. Nor any need."

"But if you were to go to London or Bath or some other place like that, you might see some of the ghosts who had been your attachments before?"

"I likely would." It was a line of questioning no other client had pursued, the second time in as many days she'd asked such insightful and unique questions.

He would have pursued the topic if not for the sudden arrival of Baby Blue. The tiny ghost wore a deeply distressed expression.

"What's happened?" Mercury asked.

"The Captain is teasing me again. I don't like when he teases me, but he keeps doing it."

"You know that one of his Integral Traits is a tendency toward tomfoolery."

"That doesn't mean he should be allowed to tease me."

Mercury hunched down a little, looking directly into that sweet little ghostly face. "You are, of course, correct. Let's go talk with him."

"I don't want to see it," Baby Blue said in an even quieter voice.

Mercury nodded slowly, knowing immediately the particular direction the Captain's teasing had taken.

He stood and offered Miss Huddleston a very brief but not insulting bow.

He began walking off the field, but Lord Garston called out to him. "You cannot abandon the game before it has reached its conclusion."

"One must question his sportsmanship," Testy Tolver said with a sniff.

"Not at all." Mercury was too well acquainted with Tolver to be at all upended by his unflattering assessments. "I am conceding. Please consider this my acceptance of my defeat." He pressed his mallet to his heart and bowed to them all.

He turned once more and continued on with Baby. While it was terribly important to keep his clients happy, he had to live in this house full of ghosts. Keeping the peace among all of them was essential.

They'd not even reached the house when Zizzy joined them. "The Captain has been teasing Baby again."

"So I've heard. Hopefully we can put an end to it, at least for a time."

The Captain would return to his teasing ways. As Granny had so aptly put it, a ghost could not help their Integral Traits.

They are looking for you. Mercury shook off her words, as he'd done countless times since she'd awoken him the night before.

The Captain popped through a garden wall directly in front of them. Just as Mercury could have predicted, he held his head in his hands. Baby shrieked.

Mercury eyed the headless haunt with exhausted exasperation. "Captain."

"What?" His tone of overdone innocence would not have fooled anyone.

"Capitate yourself," Mercury insisted.

"What is the point of having the ability to decapitate myself if I'm not allowed to do so?"

"Playing the martyr is Mawky's role," Mercury said. "You are absolutely allowed to pop your head off anytime you want, but you've been asked to stop doing it in front of Baby. You know it upsets him, and causing a child ghost distress does not reflect well on you."

Clearly annoyed, the Captain popped his head back in place. "I'm just trying to toughen the little one up."

"Baby doesn't need toughening," Mercury said. "We've had this discussion before."

"I suppose," he said with a ghostly sigh and floated back through the wall once more. From the other side, his voice echoed back. "It was far more fun on my ship."

Considering that was, as far as Mercury had been able to ascertain, a ghostly pirate ship, Mercury wasn't certain he wanted to know what form that "fun" took.

He looked down at Baby. Poor thing didn't look entirely relieved. "I don't like when he does that."

"I wish I could promise you that he won't do it again."

"I can't wait for pirate ghosts to be in fashion." Baby reached up and took hold of Zizzy's ghostly hand, and the two of them floated off. They were good for each other, even though neither of them had a figurative backbone.

Mercury rubbed at the back of his neck. He liked the Captain. And, in most respects, the sometimes-headless ghost was a good addition to the twenty. But if he kept torturing Baby, Mercury was going to have to make an effort to arrange a transfer.

He turned back, knowing he needed to rejoin the others even if he didn't rejoin the game. He needed to get Lord Garston to finally make a decision. He needed to nudge the Huddlestons toward one as well. And he needed to find out if Granny Grey was destined to prove friend or foe.

But turning back, he found Miss Huddleston was once again looking in his direction. And while she wasn't directly beside him, she was near enough that he knew she'd be able to hear him.

"While I am, I will admit, flattered," he said, "I am excessively curious as to why I so often find you looking at me."

Her brows arched, and her expression turned a little remonstrative. "And *I'm* curious why it is you think that I'm looking at *you*."

7

"Mr. Raine, you simply must go to Town for the Season," Mrs. Huddleston said as they all sat in the drawing room that evening. "With so many ghosts, you would take London by storm."

Ten of his ghosts were in the room at the moment, something she had breathlessly commented on at least a dozen times at that point. Bringing his ethereal entourage to London would be exhausting, though that wasn't the reason he refused to do so.

"I suspect the Prince Regent would grow unbearably jealous," Mercury said with a laughing grin. "For the sake of Royal Harmony, I think I'll remain at Aventine Manor."

His usual approach of humor-as-misdirection worked as it always did. Mrs. Huddleston smiled and playfully waved off his teasing. Lord Garston chuckled a little. Miss Huddleston's characteristic show of neutrality gave way to the tiniest hint of a smile. But Granny Grey, who hovered near the wall, watched him a little too knowingly.

He had to find out what she knew. He had to.

"If the Prince is so easily upset, one can only assume he is hiding something," Testy Tolver said. "Likely an Invisible attachment."

Mercury glanced at Lord Garston. The comment was undeniably judgmental, but accusing anyone of having an Invisible attachment was a shocking thing. To toss such a scandalous accusation at the heir to the throne risked being charged with treason.

"Does Testy Tolver often comment on the royal family?" Lord Garston asked.

"While I haven't heard him do so before," Mercury said, "he has not shown himself overly concerned with people's ranks or influence."

"And does he regularly accuse someone of..." Lord Garston could hardly say the words. When they did emerge, it was in a whisper. "Invisible attachments?"

"This is the first time I have heard him lob such a thing at anyone."

"Even if such an accusation were true"—Mrs. Huddleston pushed out a whoosh of air—"to say it out loud is a risky thing. An Invisible attachment is not something to be taken lightly."

It certainly wasn't. Having a ghostly attachment that couldn't be seen rendered a person suspect and untrustworthy. While no person could choose to have an Originary that was invisible, they were still held in contempt for it, and anyone who traded for one was a fool.

Lord Garston sat a little taller. "Society would enjoy the judgmentalness Tolver has just demonstrated, but I might find myself uninvited to more sophisticated gatherings if he insults people of rank."

"That is a possibility." Mercury could sense that a decision was an instant away.

"I am decided, then." Lord Garston rose as if about to address Parliament. "I choose Vernon the Vain."

Mrs. Huddleston applauded. Miss Huddleston turned her attention to Testy Tolver, her mouth bunched in concern.

"I have not yet encountered a ghost who was offended by not being selected for a swap," Mercury told her.

That she looked immediately relieved told him he'd guessed correctly what she'd been wondering. And it was to her credit that she'd been concerned for Testy Tolver's feelings.

"We should celebrate." Mrs. Huddleston jumped to her feet. "And I know the perfect way to do so: dancing!"

"Dancing?" Signora Bellona was clearly unimpressed by the suggestion.

The Quiet Queen wove her ghostly hands together and rested them on her lap, looking every bit as unamazed as the Signora sounded.

"I do enjoy an evening of dancing," Lord Garston said. "What an excellent idea."

"I'll play the pianoforte so everyone can dance." Mrs. Huddleston's gaze darted from Lord Garston to Miss Huddleston. Those two, Mercury would wager, constituted "everyone" for the purposes of the scheming mother's plans. She would discover soon enough that most of Mercury's ghosts enjoyed dancing as well.

Mrs. Huddleston suggested a jaunty country dance. Zizzy joined one of the two lines of dancers, so Mercury stood opposite her. She would feel less nervous about Lord Garston and Miss Huddleston being part of the dance if he was as well. Not *not* nervous, but *less*, Integral Traits being what they were.

The swirl of the dance really was something spectacular to see when undertaken mostly by ghosts. It was wispy and gossamer, and he couldn't blame Lord Garston and Miss Huddleston for watching it a little wide-eyed even as they attempted to continue the dance themselves. He knew ghosts did participate, to some extent, in the dancing at Society balls, but to be entirely surrounded by them in a much smaller space was awe-inspiring. He'd experienced it countless times, and he still found himself amazed by the sight.

The steps of the dance brought Zizzy and Miss Huddleston together, circling around each other.

"You are a very elegant dancer, Zizzy," Miss Huddleston said with every indication of sincerity.

A little more of Zizzy's distress melted away. Mercury didn't at all know what to think of Miss Huddleston, but that one moment inched him toward a good opinion of the lady. He smiled and hoped she saw the gratitude underlying it.

The music abruptly ended.

Mrs. Huddleston looked almost frantic. "A quadrille. Lord Garston, I'm certain you know how to dance the quadrille."

"I do." Lord Garston dipped a bow.

"My daughter dances the quadrille quite gracefully." Subtlety was not Mrs. Huddleston's specialty.

"A four-person quadrille is my particular favorite." Miss Huddleston wasn't bothering with subtlety either.

"Signora Bellona," Mrs. Huddleston said, "you likely dance quite gloriously."

"I do." The Signora floated into position.

"Vernon?" Mrs. Huddleston smiled broadly.

He accepted both the invitation and the implied compliment and took his position in the quartet.

With a quick look of relief that she didn't entirely hide, Mrs. Huddleston sat at the pianoforte once more and trilled the opening notes of a quadrille.

Far from offended, Mercury took a seat on the sofa beside Baby, who was sleeping as he usually did at this time of night—something he'd not seen any of his other ghosts do—and prepared himself to be thoroughly entertained watching the dancers. Zizzy "sat" on his other side. Granny Grey hovered behind him.

The movements of the dance brought Lord Garston and Miss Huddleston together. He took her hand as they turned. When the time came to release hands and return to their positions, Lord Garston didn't let go immediately. Not even the tiniest bit of pleasure registered on Miss Huddleston's face, though neither did she look uncomfortable or uneasy. Lord Garston was playing his hand, but she didn't seem interested in the cards he held.

"Miss Huddleston said I am an elegant dancer," Zizzy said quietly. "I think she meant it."

"You are an excellent dancer. It speaks well of her judgment that she noticed so quickly."

"Miss Huddleston is kind and thoughtful," Granny Grey said. "Her mother is overbearing, so not a lot of people get to know her well enough to realize how lovely she is."

Mercury watched as Signora Bellona flitted through the moves of the dance, ghostly chin tipped at an arrogant angle.

"And her mother wishes to swap for a ghost that is also overbearing," Granny Grey said.

Gads. He was going to have to decide how to approach this.

The Signora wouldn't care one way or the other how well matched she was to her next attachment. Neither would the Quiet Queen, if she proved the choice in the end. But Miss Huddleston might be made unhappy by either choice. Mercury would have to make absolutely certain everyone involved was truly of the same mind on the matter before anything was officially undertaken.

Miss Huddleston looked over at him, her gaze lingering. Mercury kept his eyes on her as well but leaned back and turned his head the tiniest bit toward Granny Grey.

"Miss Huddleston said that when she looks in my direction, as she's doing now," he said, "she's not necessarily looking *at me*. Do you know what she means by that?"

"That is a question best asked of her." A bit of a smile hung in the suggestion. He felt certain bashfulness was one of her Integral Traits, so he was grateful she was feeling at ease enough with him to tease a little.

"If I asked, would she actually tell me?" He looked back at the elderly ghost.

That bit of a smile he'd heard in her voice grew. "Probably not."

It seemed there was to be no end to the mysteries that the Huddlestons' arrival brought to his doorstep.

8

For the second night in a row, Mercury awoke to find a ghost at the foot of his bed, watching him. And for the second night in a row, it was not one of the current Aventine ghosts.

"Is Granny Grey going to remain at Aventine Manor?" Pearl asked with an indifferent shrug.

"If Miss Huddleston undertakes a transfer here, yes."

"Granny simply has to stay!" Pearl burst immediately into tears. Emotionally unstable ghosts had been very fashionable a year earlier. "She has to."

With a sigh of resignation, Mercury sat up in his bed and rubbed away the lingering sleep hanging heavy in his eyes.

"Why does she have to stay?" Mercury had his own reasons for wanting the geriatric ghost to remain. But until he learned Pearl's reasons, he was unlikely to get any sleep.

"Granny doesn't like London. She was unhappy there last year. And being surrounded by so many people scared her."

That rang true from all Mercury had observed of the very anxious specter. "You feel she would be more at peace here?"

The translucent tears fell faster. "So much more. So very much more."

"I am eager for Granny to reside at Aventine Manor," Mercury assured her. "And I intend to do all I can to facilitate a swap."

"You managed it with Lord Garston." Pearl's tears turned to an anxious hopefulness. "And that means I get to return to Aventine for a time."

"Which, I assure you, pleases me to no end."

Mawky floated through the wall, her hand, as always, to her heart. Her eyes darted to Mercury. "You're awake. How fortunate."

"Is it, though?" Mercury rubbed at the ache between his eyes.

"Vernon is being insufferable, and it is truly harrowing to endure." Mawky did her best to collapse dramatically on the foot of his bed but floated through it instead. "Everything is so wretched right now," she said from inside the straw mattress.

"It's very tiring, isn't it?" He managed to keep the dryness out of his tone.

Mawky's head popped up once more, though most of her remained inside his bed. "Vernon is being swapped tomorrow?"

"That is the plan."

"And Pearl will be staying here with us?"

Mercury nodded.

"After all that I have endured, this is welcome news." Though Mercury couldn't see it, he suspected there was a hand-to-heart situation taking place. "Most welcome."

"And I have every hope of Granny Grey joining our phantasmal flock in another day or two," Mercury added.

Mawky began slowly rising, more of her growing visible. "See if you can convince the Huddlestons to choose Signora Bellona." She floated closer and closer to the ceiling. "I do not know if I can bear another of her arias."

At least the Signora didn't sing in the middle of the night.

Mawky disappeared through the ceiling above. Pearl still hovered near his bed. Uncertainty and worry pulled at her ghostly features. Tears would undoubtedly return in another instant.

"Is something else weighing on you?" Perhaps he could offer some stability before she fell apart again, and, in so doing, get back to sleep that much quicker.

"I do have another Integral Trait besides emotional instability," she said.

All ghosts had more than one. "What is another of yours?"

"Intuition. I...sense things." Something in her tone had him a little on edge, a feeling of foreboding washing over him. "Granny's arrival has changed things for you. If she doesn't stay, the events she has unintentionally triggered will spiral and collapse on you."

"Does your intuition allow you to ascertain what she knows or what is coming in her wake?"

Pearl shook her head. "Only that it is coming, and without her here, it will crush you."

9

Mercury had lost count of how many ghost Transferals he had undertaken over the years. He almost never found himself distracted or surprised during a Transferal ceremony. Yet, the next day, he was decidedly both.

Distracted by Pearl's visit the night before and the warning that Granny Grey was the only thing standing between him and apparent disaster.

Surprised by Miss Huddleston entering the library in the moments before the ceremony was set to begin.

"I do not know what is acceptable or even possible," she said, looking unsure of herself. "If possible, I would like to see how a Transferal is done. If I'm to participate in the same thing, I'd prefer to have some understanding of it."

It was not only logical and reasonable, but it was also something few people thought of. She continued to surprise him in precisely that way. Clearly, Miss Huddleston had thought quite a lot about this and was curious about it all. He'd not have guessed as much during her first day at Aventine Manor. She had seemed entirely uninterested.

Mercury turned to Lord Garston, who had risen from his chair at the desk when she'd entered. "Do you have any objections to Miss Huddleston observing the Transferal?"

"None whatsoever."

Mercury waved her inside. Lord Garston welcomed her with a very broad smile. What was it that had him so interested in Miss Huddleston? The younger son of a duke could set his sights quite high. And, while Miss Huddleston seemed a fine person and her family had a significant amount of money, and she was decidedly pretty, she didn't have a title. As near as Mercury had been able to gather from eavesdropping on Mrs. Huddleston's efforts to ingratiate herself and her daughter to this prospective bridegroom, the Huddlestons didn't have any connections to nobility.

Mercury inwardly shook his head at himself. He had enough of his own difficulties without adding things that were none of his concern.

Miss Huddleston sat in a chair near them, though a bit removed. She looked at Lord Garston, Pearl, Vernon the Vain, and Mercury in turn.

Her gaze lingered longer on Mercury, though. Just as it always did.

He set his attention back on the matter at hand. Lord Garston returned to his seat and took up the quill he'd been using as he wrote out, according to the template, the agreement between them. A written and signed agreement was not *required* for Transferals, but Mercury had long ago decided that he preferred having a very specific and binding record. He could keep track of which ghost went where, of the terms of his brokerage, and he had clear proof that the swap had been agreed to by everyone.

All of that, of course, was apparent in the fact that a swap had taken place at all. But he knew from tales told to him by other brokers and some of the ghosts who had come to Aventine Manor that coercion could make a swap possible even when it was not always universally liked. Requiring people to sign documents helped lower the chances of them doing anything underhanded to instigate it.

While Lord Garston completed his portion of this, Mercury addressed the two entities involved. To Vernon the Vain, he posed the usual question first. "Vernon the Vain, are you pleased with this Transferal and willing to move forward with it?"

Vernon gave a quick and firm nod. "I've not been to London in some time. It'll be good to see what's become of the old place."

"You know I will not accept that as an answer." Any ghost who participated in a Transferal that Mercury facilitated was informed in tremendous detail that they had to give a direct yes or no. Language could be a difficult thing, and he never wanted anything to be misinterpreted.

"Yes," he said with a sniff. "I am pleased and willing to undertake this Transferal."

"And Pearl"—he turned and looked at her—"are you pleased with this Transferal and willing to move forward with it?"

She smiled. "Yes. I am both pleased and more than willing to do so."

He couldn't help but smile in return. "It'll be good to have you back at Aventine Manor for however long we're blessed to have you."

Lord Garston used his signet ring to officially sign the Transferal document. Mercury looked it over, making certain everything was in order.

"Excellent." Mercury stepped away from the desk and to the open area of the library. "We'll begin, then."

The ceremony didn't actually require any space; he simply found it easier to focus when he didn't feel closed in. The brokering part of this job was interesting and intriguing, involving doing his best to match someone with a ghost that most suited their wishes and needs while also looking out for the desires of the ghost. But the Transferal itself was taxing.

He took a breath, then another. With each exhalation he emptied his mind of other thoughts and concerns and focused entirely on his attachment to Vernon the Vain. A person with multiple attachments could feel on some level where those links were. It wasn't physical. It wasn't even mental. The connection felt impossible to explain but also impossible to mistake. Each attachment existed in a different part of that indescribable aspect of himself. And he had to find the right one in order to transfer it.

The library was very quiet, which was fortunate. He needed to deeply focus, and silence helped tremendously. He'd not needed to tell Miss Huddleston that; she seemed to sense it.

He looked over at her. There was something undeniably adorable about the way her lips twisted in thought as she watched him. She was clearly engrossed. He liked that more than he probably ought.

Mercury shook his head. He'd let thoughts of Miss Huddleston break his concentration. He needed to empty his thoughts again. He couldn't remember the last time he'd had to restart a Transferal. Miss Huddleston was upending him.

He focused again, searching through his attachments until he found Vernon's. Each broker he'd discussed this with visualized this part of the process differently. Some imagined a door opening. Others the turning of a page in a book. For Mercury, he filled his thoughts with the sight of a butterfly slowly emerging from a cocoon. It fit the experience better. Both took time. Both occurred in tiny movements. Both represented a simultaneous end and beginning.

Mercury released a slow, tense breath, bracing himself as a wave of loneliness trickled over him. That, he knew, was a universal experience for those who facilitated these switches. But no one described the feeling as intensely as he experienced it. Whether it was the result of having so many attachments or the product of a childhood filled with the agony of abandonment, he didn't know. Whatever the cause, it made these undertakings particularly exhausting.

He held his hand out and closed his eyes. He focused fiercely so he wouldn't lose hold of the attachment that was beginning to slip away. Transferal had to be perfectly synchronous.

He'd not needed to explain this part of the process to Pearl; she had undertaken it with him less than a year earlier. She set her ghostly hand in his—literally *in*. That sensation triggered the next part of the process. Just as he'd searched for the location of his attachment to Vernon, the attachment being created now was looking for its home, and he needed to stay focused until it was found.

Mercury swallowed and breathed and held himself still against the surge of desolation that accompanied this. It would last until the Transferal was complete, a process that took hours.

He didn't have to keep Pearl's hand in his for the entirety of those hours, only until he felt the new attachment begin. And it always began the same way: an instantaneous flicker of pain. He could no more identify *where* he felt the pain than he could explain *where* the ghostly attachments existed. But both were real.

That expected sting of pain snatched at him. He pulled his hand back. He opened his eyes. Breathed tightly.

"You will let me know when the Transferal is complete?" Lord Garston asked. This was not a question of impatience or dismissal. They'd done this often enough that he understood that it took some time for the process to solidify. He also knew, from experience, that it was a tiring thing for Mercury. Allowing him to have some respite while it completed was a kindness.

"I will," Mercury said.

Lord Garston bowed to him, then to Miss Huddleston.

"Will I see you at tea?" Lord Garston asked her.

She gave a small nod but didn't answer vocally. Still, it seemed enough. Lord Garston left the room, pleased as could be. Vernon and Pearl followed.

"Why did they leave with him?" Miss Huddleston asked.

Mercury sat in the chair nearest him, feeling tired already, though he had hours remaining.

"At the moment, they are both technically partially attached to him."

"But attachments don't require ghosts to remain in extreme close proximity," she said.

"During this portion of a Transferal, it does. It's a fragile connection, and they are tugged with him until it's complete."

"But they don't have to stay near *you*?"

"You have a tendency to ask me questions no one else thinks to ask," he said.

Most people, seeing this part of his brokerage services in a similar light to a merchant making a purchase or tying a package up in a neat bit of paper, found the exact mechanics of a Transferal beneath their notice. They didn't ask questions because they couldn't be bothered by the "how" of the services they purchased.

He rubbed at his temples, his energy draining already. "The number of attachments a person has remains steady, except during a Transferal. It can change for that brief time. However, a person born with an attachment can never have his or her number of attachments drop below one."

"But you, who has more than one, can temporarily lose an attachment?"

"It is, in many ways, a loss, yes."

"So, at the moment, Lord Garston has two attachments?"

Mercury nodded. "But both are, at the moment, very weakly attached to him. As I slowly exchange my attachment to Vernon and create an attachment to Pearl, his attachment to Vernon strengthens. I have to balance them both because he can't."

"And that is why you look so tired already." She spoke with the tone of one who was very quickly comprehending something but wanted to know more. "You have to manage it all, shifting and adjusting so the balance is always correct."

"I don't fully understand how it works. I don't think anyone does, but centuries of studying and pondering and various brokers leaving detailed writings have given us a lot more information than we would otherwise have."

"This is why only those with multiple attachments can facilitate Transferals; because they can release part of an attachment without their total number dropping below one." She had grasped it easily, which he appreciated. He was too worn out for deep philosophical discussions or trying to explain mechanisms he himself didn't fully understand.

He released another tight breath. *Gads*, he hated this part. Something about it dredged up memories and emotions. The unshakable feeling of being left alone was almost more than he could bear.

"Why did you choose this line of work?" she asked. "Surely there must be less difficult ways of earning a living."

"I'm certain there is, but this is something I'm able to do. And having a reliable income is not a terrible thing."

Miss Huddleston's eyes narrowed on him a little. "But it is not the whole story of why you choose it?"

"If you tell me why it is that you keep insisting you aren't looking at me when you very clearly seem to be, then perhaps I'd be willing to tell you a little more of why I have done this to myself dozens and dozens of times and intend to continue doing so."

She shook her head. "I will only say that we're all entitled to our secrets."

Granny Grey, he hoped, would be willing to share hers. Pearl insisted he was in dire straits otherwise.

"Lord Garston asked you to tell him when the Transferal is complete," Miss Huddleston said. "Does that mean you will know but he won't?"

"Only the one facilitating the Transferal feels any of this."

"I don't know what 'this' is," she said.

"We are all entitled to our secrets." He repeated her words back to her.

"May I ask another question?" she asked.

"You may ask, though I may not answer."

"Is a Transferal always difficult for the one with multiple attachments? Or is that something unique to you?"

"Every broker I've spoken to tells a similar story. It's tiring and not always pleasant, but only for the one with more than one ghost."

That seemed to give her pause. But why?

"If you're concerned that brokering a ghost swap for you will be too miserable for me, I assure you it won't be." Far from miserable—he would feel relieved.

Granny Grey *had* to stay at Aventine Manor. His entire future depended on it, as did understanding his past.

Miss Huddleston simply kept watching him. And then, without explanation or warning, she rose, gave him a quick nod and smile, then left.

That was odd indeed.

10

Mercury became slowly aware that he was not in his bed. He was waking up, but he was also *sitting* up. He kept his eyes closed, sorting out where and when he was. The puzzle was solved quickly enough by the exhaustion and lingering memory of heartbreak. That combination only ever accompanied the facilitation of a swap. He'd fallen asleep in the library waiting for the Transferal to complete.

They didn't always drain him as entirely as this one was. But he also didn't usually undertake one after having his sleep interrupted two nights in a row. He likely ought to retire to his bed early that night. With his luck of late, he'd spend half the night in sleep-heavy conversations with ghosts.

"I don't know." That was Miss Huddleston's voice.

Mercury inched his eyes open the tiniest bit and spied her standing at a distance, facing almost entirely away from him, looking at...nothing.

"I know you'd like to stay," she said to absolutely no one, "but I don't believe it's possible."

There was no one else there, person or ghost. She was very focused, her gaze not wandering in the least. And she didn't seem to be having a conversation with herself.

After a moment, she said, "For one thing, he likely could never swap you, so it would be a poor choice on his part."

Still focused. Still looking at the same spot.

She shook her head. "No, I don't think that's his only motivation, but this *is* his occupation, and he has to make wise business decisions."

Miss Huddleston was a mystery, but he didn't for a moment think she was mad. What, then, was she doing talking to the air? Air that she then followed to a slightly different location.

"We both watched the Transferal ceremony," she said. "There were words that had to be—" She shook her head. "*Saying* them didn't seem enough. They had to be *heard*."

Blast it all. In a flash, he understood not merely what he was seeing in that moment but so much about her that hadn't made sense since her arrival. And the answer wasn't at all what he could have guessed, yet it was suddenly so obvious.

Miss Huddleston had an Invisible attachment, something considered scandalous, undesirable, and even dangerous.

"He's *what*?" She snapped her head in his direction as her eyes pulled wide.

Mercury propped an elbow on the arm of the chair and rubbed at his chin with his upturned hand. "Now this," he said, "is very interesting."

He meant the remark far more playfully than she clearly interpreted it. The terror that entered her eyes brought him quickly to his feet.

He held his hands up in what he hoped would be seen as a gesture of reassurance. "I don't hold to the universal disapproval of Invisibles."

Her eyes darted around as if expecting to see someone suddenly there watching and listening. But they were alone... other than the ghost he couldn't see, that was. Still, he could understand her worry, and he didn't intend to add to it.

Invisible attachments were almost always viewed as threatening, and those who had them were subject to everything from ostracism to culpability in any horrible thing that could possibly be laid at their feet, warranted or otherwise.

"Your mother doesn't know?" he guessed.

She shook her head. "My father knew, but he warned me not to ever allow Mother to discover the truth." Her eyes drifted a bit away, focusing just behind him. She nodded, seemingly in response to something.

"This is why you said you weren't actually looking at me when you were looking in my direction."

"He thinks you are very intriguing," she said. "I am forever finding him hovering near you."

He tried to match the direction of her gaze. "Welcome to Aventine Manor."

Miss Huddleston didn't look entirely appeased, but some of her panic had ebbed. "He says, 'Thank you.' And he hopes that you will not spill this secret. He understands that it's dangerous."

"So do I," Mercury reassured the spot where he assumed the Invisible was hovering. "I hope you know you are free to make yourself at home while you are here."

Miss Huddleston twitched a brief smile to her unseen companion.

"I am not at all versed in Invisible attachments," Mercury said. "No one speaks of them, for obvious reasons. Can other ghosts see him? Obviously, the only *person* who can is you."

"I am the only one, person or ghost, who can see or hear him. As far as I can tell, no one can even sense him nearby."

That seemed like a very lonely existence. And it must be very tiring for Miss Huddleston to keep such a perilous secret.

"Does my mother have to be present for a Transferal ceremony?" she asked.

"For your first one, yes."

She rubbed at her forehead. "Is the ceremony different when both people involved have more than one attachment?"

He nodded. "It *is* a little different. And even someone who has never seen a Transferal before would likely be able to tell what was happening."

Miss Huddleston met and held his gaze. "Then I can't move forward with this. If I do, my mother will know something that I cannot risk her discovering."

"You won't make a Transferal?" He needed her to. Desperately. Granny Grey had to stay at Aventine. Too much depended on that.

"I cannot," she said. "I absolutely cannot."

11

Mercury didn't join his guests for dinner that evening, which was unusual for him even on Transferal days. He always pushed through any lingering exhaustion for the sake of keeping his clients happy enough to return for future swaps. But that day he had more to worry about than whether Lord Garston was required to take his after-dinner port alone.

Miss Huddleston didn't mean to allow a swap. Granny Grey, then, wouldn't be staying. Mercury needed a plan, and for the first time in more years than he could recall, he couldn't come up with one. In fact, he gave up trying and made his way to the drawing room not long after the others.

He dipped his head to all of his guests as he stepped inside. "My apologies for being absent during dinner. I trust your meal was to your liking."

Mrs. Huddleston beamed at him. "Every meal at Aventine Manor has been delicious. Best not let word of this reach London or someone will attempt to steal your chef."

Mercury held back a grin. Should anyone attempt to do so, he wished them a great deal of luck. The situation was far more...interesting than most would guess.

Mrs. Huddleston, Lord Garston, Weeping William, and Miss Huddleston sat at a table engaged in a game of whist. He'd been told by clients that specters who could manipulate physical things often participated in card games at Society gatherings. There were, however, rules against ghosts doing so at gambling dens.

"Pearl has wandered off," Lord Garston said as he studied his cards. "I assumed that means the Transferal is complete."

"It is." Mercury sat on a sofa that faced the table. Baby was sleeping atop it, his usual approach to evenings.

"Excellent," Mrs. Huddleston said. "You and Vernon will cut quite a dash this Season, Lord Garston."

"I will make note of anyone who doesn't recognize as much." Vernon sniffed in palatable disapproval.

"I hope you aren't leaving too soon," Mrs. Huddleston said. "We're having such a lovely time."

"I know this is your very first ghost exchange," Lord Garston said. "I would not abandon you when you are undertaking something so new. I will happily remain at Aventine Manor to offer my support and encouragement."

Years of practice enabled Mercury to hide the twinge of annoyance he felt. But if there was any chance Lord Garston's presence would help encourage a swap to actually occur, he welcomed the assistance.

Granny Grey had to stay.

"Perhaps we might travel together to London afterward," Mrs. Huddleston said.

"Does this mean you've chosen your new ghost?" Lord Garston asked.

Through it all, Miss Huddleston's eyes darted from her mother to Lord Garston and back again, over and over.

"Signora Bellona will be absolutely perfect," Mrs. Huddleston said. "And, dare I say, she and Vernon the Vain would make quite an impression arriving at Society gatherings together."

Again, Mrs. Huddleston proved she'd not ever learned the meaning of, let alone the value of, subtlety.

"Oh, what a picture they would make." Lord Garston warmed immediately to the idea.

Miss Huddleston, however, did not. "Mother, we haven't discussed this."

Mrs. Huddleston waved that off. "It is the perfect choice. She is beautiful and elegant—"

"Yes, I am," the Signora said. "There are many who think they are, but are decidedly lacking in such things."

Mrs. Huddleston's excitement only grew. "And she is so fashionably judgmental."

"I don't know that I want a fashionable ghost," Miss Huddleston said.

Mercury knew that what she actually didn't want was for her mother to learn a few things that a Transferal would reveal. The shocked silence that followed Miss Huddleston's declaration would likely only have been *more* pointed if she had revealed her true reason for not wanting to move forward.

The ghosts in the room reacted in the expected way. Some looked worried, others amused. There were tears. Disapproval. Baby kept sleeping.

Through tight lips, Mrs. Huddleston said, "We have a chance to obtain such an impressive one. Surely you must be excited at an opportunity few are afforded."

"We have not felt the need to have a fashionable ghost in the past," Miss Huddleston said.

Clearly frustrated, her mother muttered, "You weren't *twenty-five* in the past."

A quick glance at Granny Grey revealed her usual worry. Weeping William was predictably weeping. Gary the Green looked thoroughly annoyed. Captain Capitate had popped his head off again. There'd be chaos soon enough.

"A Transferal isn't possible if the one with the attachment doesn't want to make the swap," he said. "Even if an attempt is made, it won't take effect."

Miss Huddleston and Granny Grey flashed him nearly identical looks of alarm and warning. For her part, Miss Huddleston actually looked a little angry.

Though it had not been his intention, it seemed he had made the situation worse. He didn't often misjudge interactions with people or specters. Granny Grey, Pearl, and Miss Huddleston had him entirely upended.

With the stiff dignity of a statue, Mrs. Huddleston rose, necessitating that Mercury and Lord Garston stand as well. "I would like to have a word with my daughter." Her voice turned a little more dulcet, and her expression a little more pleasant when she looked at Lord Garston. "I hope you will forgive me for disrupting our game." She looked over at Mercury, and her expression hardened a little again. "And I hope you will forgive me for asking you to leave your own drawing room when you have only just arrived."

He dipped his head before walking with unhurried but not noticeably dragging steps from the room. Lord Garston continued down the corridor with Vernon, the two of them discussing people they would likely see and places they would likely visit during the Season.

Granny Grey was hovering near Mercury in the corridor, which gave him a chance to speak with her.

"I hadn't intended to add fuel to the fire," he said.

Granny Grey shook her head. "What you said was, in almost every other circumstance, perfectly reasonable and acceptable. Mrs. Huddleston tends to be short on patience when her back has been put up. She'll browbeat her daughter. It is her usual approach."

That was what Mercury was concerned about.

"I cannot, in good conscience, facilitate a Transferal someone has been pressured into. What I said was true: it cannot be completed if either of the people involved is not in favor of it. But a person can be coerced, can have their arm twisted enough that they accept it. There are unscrupulous brokers who will take advantage of that, but I don't care to be one of them."

"I believe you," Granny Grey said.

"But I don't know the Huddlestons well enough to necessarily be able to recognize the difference between Miss Huddleston genuinely deciding she wants to move forward and Mrs. Huddleston forcing the matter."

Though Granny Grey's posture never was truly stooped, something in it grew more firm and steady. "Miss Huddleston has backbone."

"I want you to stay at Aventine," he told Granny Grey. "But I don't want Miss Huddleston to agree to such a thing only because she wants to keep the peace." Granny Grey might not know about Miss Huddleston's Invisible. He didn't wish to reveal a secret that wasn't his to tell.

"Living with her mother has taught her the benefit of 'keeping the peace,' as you put it. But I don't think her hand will be forced in this."

"Which puts us in a difficult situation," he said. "I suspect you know why I am anxious for you to remain here."

Granny Grey nodded. "And I would like to stay, but there's only one way for that to be accomplished."

"Is there any chance you would tell me what you hinted at if you *didn't* stay here?"

She didn't answer out loud, but the enormous hesitancy that entered her expression told him he would not hear even another syllable of what she'd hinted at without her residence switching to his home.

In the very next moment, Mrs. Huddleston swept past him, all offended dignity, but also worryingly pleased with herself. Signora Bellona floated alongside her, their expressions very nearly identical.

Mercury met the eye of Aventine Manor's operatic torturer. He lifted a brow in inquiry.

The Signora sniffed. "She's a stubborn girl. I like that."

Stubborn. That likely meant Miss Huddleston hadn't bowed to her mother's pressure. At least not yet.

Mercury returned to the drawing room. Baby had awoken and was sitting on the sofa, looking concerned.

"Don't fret," he told the poor little sprite. "All will be well. You need to rest." Someday he would solve the mystery of why this ghost slept when he'd never met or heard of any others who did.

He turned back to Miss Huddleston, doing a quick assessment. She looked a little weary but not defeated.

"She didn't convince you?" Mercury asked.

"Refusing is far too crucial." She offered no more explanation, no doubt because of the other ghosts present. Her secret was too dangerous;

he understood that. "But she will grow more forceful and make things more miserable. I don't know what to do."

"Keep refusing, I suppose."

"It isn't that simple," she said. "I am an unmarried woman. The very fabric of Society requires those in my position to be dependent on others. For that reason, I am dependent on my mother. I have nowhere to go other than her home, no one I can rely on but her. And she has a voice and, to a degree, a vote in the Transferal of my attachment, and I can't escape that."

"I learned a few lessons as a child," Mercury said, "most of them unpleasant." He could feel Granny Grey's gaze on him as he made that admission. He didn't dare look at her. There were so many questions he wanted to ask that he could not yet have answers to. Worse than that, he suspected he didn't necessarily want them all. "One thing I learned was that the solutions to the most complicated problems are usually the ones most worth finding."

"They also are often the hardest to discover," she pointed out.

"Would it be worth finding an answer to this one?" he asked her.

She nodded without hesitation, without flinching, without looking beaten down. She was in a difficult situation, and she acknowledged it. But, as Granny Grey had so aptly pointed out, she had a backbone. She was most certainly going to need it. They both were.

12

Aventine Manor held nearly as many secrets as Mercury himself. How many of those secrets had been uncovered by his ghosts, he didn't know. But only Baby, Zizzy, and Smythe knew where he'd come from and who he was. His other seventeen Originaries knew they had once been attached to an orphan, but they didn't know what name he used now. And none of them had known how many attachments he had. The moment he'd discovered none of them knew the total number, he'd seen his chance for freedom.

Of all the ghosts he'd traded attachments to, only one knew anything even approaching the entirety of what he kept hidden: The Scholar. And, in a bit of inarguable irony, one of the things kept hidden at Aventine Manor was…The Scholar.

Long after the house had descended into the quiet peacefulness of night, Mercury lit a tall candle and carried it in a sturdy silver candlestick. He pushed open the trick bookshelf at the east end of the library and stepped through to the hidden winding stairs beyond. The shelf slid back into place behind him as he climbed.

His home was quite literally swarming with ghosts who were all entirely capable of and more than willing to float through walls and ceilings, exploring to their wispy hearts' content. Yet, The Scholar had told him that none had ever discovered his attic room. And he preferred it that way. The Scholar liked his peaceful nook. He never left it and never seemed at all inclined to do so. And Mercury had never heard him express any desire for the other ghosts to learn of his whereabouts or even his existence. A preference for quiet isolation very much appeared to be one of The Scholar's Integral Traits.

Mercury reached The Scholar's door and lightly knocked.

"You're always welcome, Mercury," came the usual response in the usual Irish accent.

He stepped inside, knowing precisely what he would see: stacks of books and papers, a large, dust-covered desk with a cozy leather chair, and a ghost in the robes of academia with spectral spectacles resting on the tip of his pointed nose, "sitting" behind the desk.

"It's been some time since we had a late-night meeting of the minds," The Scholar said.

Mercury sat in the only other chair in the room, the one he always used during these visits. "Have you missed me?"

With a little smile acknowledging the quip, The Scholar asked, "What's brought you up the stairs tonight?"

"I have a seemingly unanswerable quandary. As you are the wisest ghost I know, wiser than probably any *person* I've ever met, I think you might be the only one capable of helping me sort this out."

"I do enjoy a challenging puzzle." The Scholar took off his ghostly glasses and eyed Mercury with quizzical excitement.

"One of my favorite things about having you here." Mercury set his candle on the desk. "This is a complicated situation, made more difficult by the fact that I am not in a position to tell you everything about it—some aspects are not my secrets to share."

The Scholar nodded ponderously. "Share what you *are* able."

Mercury leaned back in his chair. "I have a new client and her mother here: Miss and Mrs. Huddleston. The mother is overbearing and, I'm beginning to suspect, harmfully controlling. The daughter isn't unwilling to make a swap, not even opposed to it. She simply doesn't want to do so with her mother present."

"Why not?" The Scholar asked.

"That is one of those things I'm not in a position to share with you."

The Scholar nodded and motioned for him to continue.

"The mother will, without question, demand she continue with the trade and will demand to know why it doesn't happen, if it doesn't, or make her daughter miserable if they leave Aventine Manor without the new ghost she, herself, selected."

"You think the daughter will hold to her refusal?"

"I do." Mercury couldn't imagine Miss Huddleston would reveal her Invisible attachment. No amount of browbeating was likely to convince her to spill that secret to a mother she had admitted she didn't trust.

"You seem particularly concerned about her not undertaking the Transferal you anticipated. Your reasons are likely more than a concern about her mother rendering her miserable."

"I have reason to want...*need*, really, her current attachment to stay at Aventine Manor."

"And it isn't that Miss Huddleston is opposed to ghost swaps on the whole?"

Mercury shook his head.

"And her ghost does not object."

"You know me better than to believe I would attempt to force a ghost to agree to an exchange."

A slow, calm nod answered that reminder. "So the core difficulty is that Miss Huddleston won't participate in a Transferal if her mother is present for the ceremony."

"This would be Miss Huddleston's first Transferal. Immediate family members of the same household *have* to be present. It can't even be done otherwise."

"Why doesn't she want her mother there? Being overbearing doesn't seem a reason to need her to be absent."

"I cannot tell you that."

His ghostly eyes narrowed. "Why do you need her ghost to remain?"

"I cannot tell you that either." *Can't* was probably not the correct word. That matter wasn't Miss Huddleston's secret; it was his. But keeping his origins and his fugitive status out of public knowledge was crucial. Only his three remaining Originaries knew who he had once been.

"How essential is it that this ghost remains at Aventine Manor?" The Scholar asked.

"Quite essential. Potentially life-altering."

"Life-*ruining*?" The Scholar pressed.

"Potentially."

"Allow me to summarize: It is crucial for you that Miss Huddleston's ghost remain. Her ghost cannot remain without being traded. This ghost cannot be traded without *Mrs.* Huddleston present. Miss Huddleston won't undertake a Transferal if her mother is present. Thus, her ghost cannot remain."

"An excellent summary of my very frustrating situation."

"If all of those things are true—"

"They are."

"And each part of that chain is intrinsically connected to the rest?"

Mercury nodded.

"If all the pieces of that puzzle are true and intrinsically connected to the rest, then one of the two of you will not get what you want." The Scholar returned his spectacles to their place on his narrow nose. "Either Miss Huddleston will be required to undertake a Transferal with her mother present, or you will not be able to have her ghost remain at Aventine Manor."

Mercury stood, pacing the cluttered space as best he could manage. *Granny's arrival has changed things for you. If she doesn't stay, the events she has unintentionally triggered will spiral and collapse on you.*

"There has to be a third option," he said tightly. "There has to be."

"The only way to obtain a different outcome is to break the chain, Mercury Raine."

"How do you know breaking it is even possible?" Mercury asked.

"How do you know it *isn't*?"

Mercury paced and pondered. *Break the chain.* Could it even be done? If so, where? How?

"Granny Grey—that's Miss Huddleston's ghost—cannot be more than five hundred feet from her so long as Granny is Miss Huddleston's attachment. That cannot be changed." He turned, beginning another circuit of the studious attic space. "A first Transferal *has* to be done with the approval and in the presence of all immediate family members living in the household of the one with the attachment. That also cannot be changed."

"Could Miss Huddleston's mind be changed about not wanting her mother present?"

"Absolutely not." And Mercury couldn't blame her.

"Then it is the mother that needs to be sorted," The Scholar said. "Remove her from the equation, and the outcome changes."

"She is an immediate family member—"

"Something that cannot be changed," The Scholar acknowledged.

"—in the same household," Mercury finished. "That means she has to—" *Oh.*

Oh.

"If they don't live in the same household," Mercury said, thinking out loud, "then her mother is no longer part of the Transferal ceremony."

The Scholar smiled kindly. "The weak link in the chain."

"And my sought-for answer." Mercury took up his candle. "The start of it, at least. An unmarried lady doesn't have a lot of options in terms of her household. She cannot simply shrug and tell her mother she's setting up house somewhere."

"She could if she is getting married," The Scholar said.

"Mrs. Huddleston does seem to want her daughter to make a match with Lord Garston." Mercury shook his head. "But Miss Huddleston will refuse that just as adamantly as she will a Transferal with her mother present."

"If *you* marry her," The Scholar said, "Aventine Manor will be her home, and *you* will be her immediate family living in her household. Will that answer the difficulty with the Transferal?"

"Technically, yes. But it would create an entire slew of other troubles." For one thing, he'd have to use his legal name for any wedding to be binding, and he wasn't willing to reveal that. For another, he had no desire to tie himself to a lady he didn't love who didn't love him. For another, he suspected Miss Huddleston wouldn't have him. His respect for her only grew at the realization. "Marriage is not a viable solution."

"Then your focus must be on her establishing a household free of her mother," The Scholar said. "Something nearly impossible for an unmarried lady of marriageable age. Any money she might have will be controlled by her mother or trustees, preventing her from accessing it in order to obtain lodgings."

That was entirely true. "She would need a place to live for free, which is unlikely to happen. Few people have extra houses available to simply hand over to a friend."

"You do." The Scholar eyed him over his spectacles.

"Larissa Lodge," Mercury Raine realized in a whoosh of breath. "But it is so closely tied to Aventine Manor. There is likely to be a scandal."

"Closely tied, but *part of*. That is not an insignificant difference." The Scholar leaned back in his chair.

"Society would not permit her to live alone, regardless." Yet, Mercury felt he was quite close to the answer he was seeking. "There must be something I'm missing or not thinking of."

"Most likely." The Scholar bent over his book once more. "But you are at least closer to a solution."

Mercury crossed to the door. He was unlikely to sleep that night. His mind would spin, attempting to find the bits and pieces that would make the idea a viable one.

"Bear in mind," The Scholar said from his desk, "you do intend to ask her to make a monumental change in her life so that you can have a ghost that you desperately need for reasons you won't disclose. That, Mercury Raine, requires you to trust her. And trust isn't something you are precisely known for."

13

Mercury checked every place in Aventine Manor he could think of the next morning, but he couldn't find Miss Huddleston. His path crossed with Lord Garston and *Mrs.* Huddleston in the east sitting room, and he quickly ascertained why her daughter was playing least in sight.

"My daughter is, as you discovered, quite a graceful dancer," Mrs. Huddleston said to her lordly conversational companion. "And the ladies of Society simply adore her."

"If she has not yet formally been introduced to my mother, I would be honored to make that introduction."

"How very gallant of you, Lord Garston." A flash of embarrassed uncertainty entered her eyes. "I am certain my daughter is somewhere nearby."

Mercury, listening unseen from the doorway, was increasingly certain she was intentionally *not* nearby. Where, then, was she?

He stepped away from the sitting room in search of the elusive young lady. Fate had seldom been kind to him but chose to be in that moment. He crossed paths with Zizzy.

"You haven't happened to have seen Miss Huddleston, have you? I suspect she's hiding from..." He simply raised a brow.

Zizzy responded with a look of absolute empathy. "I saw her on the grounds, keeping herself tucked behind walls and shrubbery."

Hiding, and with good reason.

"Would you show me where on the grounds you saw her?"

She nodded and floated alongside him as he made his way outside. "I like Miss Huddleston. She is very kind to me."

"That makes me like her a little as well."

"Only a little?" Zizzy didn't approve of that.

"I only know her *a little*," he reminded Zizzy.

She nodded. "And you don't warm to people quickly."

"With good reason."

Zizzy motioned ahead to the small alcove in the walled garden. "She was in there when I last saw her."

Mercury peeked inside, and sure enough, she was walking along the gravel path that wound through it.

"Will her mother make her unhappy again?" Zizzy asked, anxiety dripping from her.

"Not if we can help it."

"I will place myself between here and the house," Zizzy said. "I'll hurry over should her mother or Lord Garston come in this direction."

"An excellent plan." Mercury stepped into the walled garden.

Miss Huddleston spotted him quickly. "Are you alone?"

He lowered his eyes, shaking his head as if humiliated. "Even Zizzy has abandoned me."

"She is entirely devoted to you, Mercury Raine. She wouldn't abandon you."

"You have caught me out. She is actually standing guard to make certain your mother and your would-be suitor don't bother you here."

"I *might* actually be tempted to allow a Transferal if I could have Zizzy with me."

If only she knew that Zizzy didn't have any desire to leave, and Mercury was not going to press the matter when it was such a sensitive topic for the tender-hearted specter.

Miss Huddleston tossed him a pointed look. "I'm not *actually* considering undertaking a Transferal, you realize. It is too great a risk."

"And what would you say if I told you I think there's a chance you will change your mind about that?" Seeing worry creep into her expression, he quickly explained, "I have an idea that would allow you to make your first Transferal without your mother present."

"I thought that was impossible."

"In your current circumstances, it is. Immediate family members in your household have to be present and in approval. The why isn't known, but centuries of documentation and failed attempts to circumvent it confirm that it is absolutely true."

She was watching him closely as they walked on.

"But immediate family members who do not reside in the same household as the one undertaking a first Transferal have no say in the matter, and their presence is not required. If you do not share a household with your mother..." He let the rest of the realization dangle.

Miss Huddleston looked intrigued but also discouraged. "I am an unmarried lady. We do not have most of the options that gentlemen do. Even if I had a house at my disposal, I do not have any income. And even if I had income, living alone without so much as a lady's companion would cause an enormous scandal. I am dependent upon my mother for my existence in every conceivable way, and that gives her control over most aspects of my life."

Mercury had pondered those exact difficulties for hours the night before.

"I had a client a couple of years ago who undertook a trade specifically because her ghost at the time was a child, and this client was in need of a companion so she could live on her own."

"Society accepted her attachment as a reasonable lady's companion?"

Mercury nodded. "I heard from other clients that the arrangement was working well. A ghost with the right demeanor seemed to satisfy expectations."

"I would need to make certain I always traded for ghosts who could serve in that function, I suppose."

They were getting somewhere. "Do you have any friends you could live with?"

"My mother has always kept me very isolated. I have never had the opportunity for acquaintances to become true friends."

That had, no doubt, helped her keep her Invisible a secret. But it was still a cruel thing for a mother to do.

"I think the issue of income is likely the one that will have to be solved first," Miss Huddleston said. "Income would allow me to both place a roof over my head *and* eat while under that roof. I am not ashamed to admit that I prefer being able to do both."

Her dry tone brought a smile to his face. He'd been in the position of being unsure how to obtain a home and not starve. If not for his ability to broker—

Blazes. The ability to broker. That might be the answer.

He took a quick glance around, needing to be absolutely certain they were alone. He dropped his voice low. "You have more than one attachment. That means you could be a ghost broker, which would give you an income."

She pondered it, brow pulling. "But wouldn't that at least hint at the fact that I have an Invisible attachment? I can't risk people sorting that out."

"That *is* a difficulty," he acknowledged. "I don't think anyone has ever seen all of my ghosts at one time, but no one has ever assumed any of them are Invisibles. If you operated in the countryside rather than London, where you'd be under more scrutiny, people might simply assume that your other attachment is bashful or misanthropic."

"Perhaps." Miss Huddleston's mouth twisted and pulled as they continued their circuit. Her gaze lingered a moment on Larissa Lodge as they passed it. She stopped, her mouth twisting in that adorable look of pondering he'd come to like. "Is Larissa Lodge within five hundred feet of Aventine Manor?"

He nodded. "Yes, though only just."

"And you own it?"

He nodded again. "It is, technically, no longer part of the Aventine Manor estate, but it does belong to me." That had been reason for hesitancy when The Scholar had suggested it as a possible residence for Miss Huddleston. It was connected to an unattached gentleman who wasn't family to her.

"Have you ever considered renting it?" She held his gaze. "My ghost could mingle with yours, and no one would know that I was involved in the brokering at all. That would nearly eliminate the risk of people guessing at my situation."

Renting it would help the situation be less scandalous. Having a tenant was not the same as "keeping" a woman.

Mercury rubbed at his mouth as he thought it through. "It would make transfers a little more complicated but not impossible. And having a lady to take tea with or walk about the grounds with would help put some of my more uncertain female clients a little more at ease, which would help my brokerage business. And making certain it is known that you are renting the lodge would help squelch any unfavorable whispers."

"You realize what you are describing sounds almost like a partnership."

It did. And that wasn't quite what he'd bargained for. Yet, it would allow him to have Granny Grey at Aventine Manor, which was crucial.

"I also feel I have to remind you," she said, "that I have no idea how to facilitate a Transferal. I would need to be trained."

She would be a neighbor. A business partner. A protégée. For one person to be connected to him in all three of those ways required that he take a risk and that he trust her, and trust was, as The Scholar had rightly pointed out, not his specialty.

Granny Grey's late-night confession, combined with Pearl's late-night warning, pushed him forward. He couldn't afford to let Granny slip away. Far too much was at stake.

A partnership. One that would save his business, his ghosts, and himself.

"I can train you," he said. "And we can sort out a way of making this partnership work."

"Which leaves us with one last difficulty." She sighed, sounding exceptionally tired. "The law gives my mother the ability to make things deeply difficult for me if I simply attempt to walk away or leave home. I don't know how to convince her to allow me to do so."

"Perhaps 'allow' isn't the right approach."

"You're suggesting I run away from home?" she asked with a laugh.

Run away. The past twelve hours had been filled with unexpected moments of budding brilliance and half-formed ideas. It seemed his mind was not yet done formulating them. Another thought tickled at the back of his brain. "Hmmm."

She looked back at him again. "That was a very intriguing 'hmmm.'"

"I have the beginnings of what is likely to prove an utterly odd but potentially brilliant idea."

"It would allow me to set up house at Larissa Lodge?" she asked.

He nodded.

"And my mother couldn't prevent it or drag me back to her home?"

"She cannot snatch hold of you if she doesn't know where you are," he said.

Miss Huddleston stopped their slow circuit of the garden and looked directly at him. "Are you suggesting I spend my life in hiding?"

He shook his head. "What I am about to suggest is far more complicated."

14

"That frustrating daughter of mine had best agree to a Transferal quickly," Mrs. Huddleston muttered, watching Lord Garston's carriage roll away from Aventine Manor. "This fish won't stay on the hook long."

Mercury was well-versed in the art of not laughing when doing so wouldn't serve his purpose, no matter how entertaining a situation was. He sat casually in a chair in the drawing room, hiding the fact that he was watching the lady closely. He needed to make certain she saw what he and Miss Huddleston needed her to see.

"Mr. Raine." Smythe floated in through the doorway.

"Yes, Smythe." Mercury suspected he knew what he was about to be told.

"Zizzy has expressed concern that Miss Huddleston did not meet her on the grounds for a walk they had arranged to undertake together this morning."

"Perhaps Miss Huddleston is simply getting a late start," Mercury suggested.

"Mawky peeked into Miss Huddleston's room, and it is empty, sir." Smythe was not at all required to refer to Mercury as "sir," but had insisted on doing so from the moment he had excitedly assumed the role of butler.

"Empty?" Mrs. Huddleston's forehead creased, and her mouth turned down sharply.

"Miss Huddleston was not inside?" Mercury asked.

"She was not, and neither were any of her belongings."

"*All* her belongings are gone?" Mrs. Huddleston's confusion didn't bode overly well for the plot he'd hatched with her daughter. For it to work, Mrs. Huddleston needed to come to the conclusion they were nudging her toward without realizing they were doing so. "We have not decided on a departure date. Why would she have packed her belongings already?"

"Not merely packed, but removed from the premises." Mercury pretended to be intrigued and confused. "Would she have sent her things onward without her?"

Mrs. Huddleston made a ponderous noise and walked with purposeful steps from the drawing room. Mercury followed behind at a distance. Baby joined him halfway to their destination.

"Is Miss Huddleston in danger?" Baby asked.

"I'm certain she is perfectly fine." He and Miss Huddleston had decided it was best not to share the plan with all the ghosts until after it proved successful. Only Smythe knew.

Mrs. Huddleston stopped a few steps inside her daughter's guest chamber and looked around in confused horror. "She truly is gone."

"As is Lord Garston," Smythe said with a pointed look. "One must wonder at the coincidence."

"If you are suggesting that my daughter would elope with—" She didn't finish. Her brow furrowed. Confusion warred with realization, which, in turn, swirled into a hint of avarice. "Elope with—" Satisfaction was the emotion she eventually settled on.

"Has Miss Huddleston run off with Lord Garston after all?" Mercury watched her with ill-disguised, and entirely feigned, shock.

"Certainly not." But Mrs. Huddleston looked hopeful.

"We will leave you to do your packing, Mrs. Huddleston," Smythe said, floating back out of the room.

"Do tell me if you need anything," Mercury said.

"'Packing'? 'Need anything'?" Was Mrs. Huddleston going to have to be led all the way to the needed conclusion when it had already been laid out in front of her? Good heavens.

Baby, despite not knowing what was happening under the surface, came to the rescue. "To go after your daughter, of course. She's run off with a man!"

"Of course. Of course." Though Mrs. Huddleston made the acknowledgment with every indication that she intended to follow through, she left the room so slowly one would think she was a Society matron hoping to linger long enough to hear a particularly scandalous bit of gossip.

Mercury didn't have to think long to sort out why. If she waited long enough, Mrs. Huddleston could insist that the lord marry her daughter, which would make all her wildest dreams come true. It was a helpful development: if she pursued slowly, she wouldn't catch up for some time, which would hide the real situation.

"Again, do send word if you find yourself in need of anything." Mercury gave a bow and made absolutely certain his expression contained just the right amount of nonchalance and a willingness to be scandalized at what might come next.

They had reached the critical juncture at which the plan he'd hatched with Miss Huddleston would either work brilliantly or fall to bits. Mrs. Huddleston's willingness to delay her departure a little to ensure Lord Garston remained far enough ahead of her for a marriage with her daughter to be all but guaranteed bought some needed time, but it also meant an increased risk of her realizing what was actually happening at Aventine Manor.

Smythe would reveal nothing. If Mercury weren't near to hand, Mrs. Huddleston couldn't ask questions of him. And his pointed absence would only further convince the meddling mother that she had a scandal to see to.

Excellent.

Mercury casually made his way from the house, grateful Mrs. Huddleston had been placed in a room facing the front grounds. She wouldn't spy him making his way across the back lawn and around the walled garden. And she wouldn't see him knock on the door of Larissa Lodge. Neither would she spy who it was that opened the door.

"Has the plan worked?" Miss Huddleston asked.

"Thus far."

She motioned him inside.

"Your mother will be in pursuit of Lord Garston in another hour or two, I imagine," he said. "And I get the impression she doesn't intend to catch him quickly."

"How touchingly maternal of her," Miss Huddleston said dryly.

"We'll keep your presence hidden until after she inevitably returns looking for you," he said, "but you would still do well to think of a different name to use when you begin taking part in this brokerage partnership."

"I already have," she said. "Tacey Wilde."

An interesting choice. "Why that name?"

She shook her head. "We are all entitled to our secrets."

"You say that to me a lot, Miss Tacey Wilde," he said.

She simply shrugged.

His gaze happened upon Granny Grey in that moment, hovering in a doorway on the other side of the room. "Are you unhappy with this arrangement?" he asked the specter.

"No," she said. "Provided Miss H—Miss Wilde continues to be happy here." There was a warning in the declaration.

"I never require anyone, be they person or ghost, to participate in things that will make them unhappy nor be part of anything dangerous if they aren't both aware of the risks and fully willing to take them." He offered the reassurance to both Granny and the newly christened Miss Wilde at the same time. "This arrangement is rife with pitfalls."

"I know," Miss Wilde said. "But ones I am willing to navigate."

"Settle yourself in as best you can without drawing notice," Mercury said. "Once your mother has left Aventine Manor for good, we can begin the work of establishing your new identity."

"And my instruction in brokering ghosts?" she pressed.

He nodded. That bit would be both tricky and interesting. Above all, it would be a challenge. And he loved a challenge.

As predicted, Mrs. Huddleston returned to Aventine Manor the next day. She very pointedly didn't admit that she hadn't found her daughter in company with Lord Garston. Her less-than-expert efforts to discover, without being obvious about it, if Miss Huddleston remained in the area left her noticeably disappointed. Her departure disappointed *no one*.

The newly christened Miss Wilde would need to undertake a change in appearance in addition to her change in name. That would have to be part of her training period. She would learn the mechanics of Transferals as well as the business of it. Granny Grey would be in proximity, and Mercury might learn a little more about the mystery of Invisibles.

And the mystery of himself.

Late in the evening, the day after Mrs. Huddleston had taken herself off for good, Mercury crossed paths with Granny Grey. "How is Miss Wilde faring at Larissa Lodge?" he asked.

"I think she's overwhelmed but also beside herself with excitement. You've offered her freedom."

"You sound surprised."

"I am." She, unsurprisingly, looked immediately anxious. "It's more than I expected you to manage."

Mercury just smiled. He wasn't bothered by doubts or criticisms.

"I didn't think you'd be able to find a way for me to remain at Aventine Manor if Miss Hudd—Miss Wilde didn't agree to a Transferal," Granny Grey admitted.

"I was extremely motivated to keep you here," he said.

"Because you are afraid of what I know?"

"A little." His secrets were dangerous things, and not merely for himself. "But also because I have been told that difficulties are coming my way, and that you, Granny Grey, are essential to my ability to navigate them."

"More than mere difficulties," Granny Grey said. "It is a storm, a collision of past and future, with you caught in the eye."

"You said you knew my name isn't Mercury Raine. Do you know, then, what it originally was?"

She smiled knowingly. "Even you don't know that."

And with that, he had one piece of his puzzle, something he hadn't known before. All his life he'd wondered if the name he'd had at the orphanage had been chosen by his parents or by the head of that miserable institution. No one there would tell him.

But Granny Grey knew, and she had just told him.

He didn't know his true name. A clue to his identity. A part of himself he wouldn't have known otherwise.

Mercury likely ought to have felt threatened by Granny's knowledge of such a dangerous secret. But, to his surprise, he didn't.

"You told me that first night that there are other ghosts who know things about me."

"Bits and pieces, yes," Granny said. "Snippets stretched out between us all."

"How?"

"I don't know." There was no doubting her sincerity. She truly didn't know how she knew what she did. "And I can't explain how I am aware that the others exist or that their paths are destined to bring them here. But it is true."

Destined to arrive at Aventine. Keys to his past. Threats to his future. "They are looking for me?"

She nodded. "And now you can be looking for them. Gather them, and all those scattered pieces will be together for the first time in your life."

"The answer to who I am." The realization spilled almost breathlessly from him.

"An answer that will change things."

"For me?"

"For your ghosts. For Miss Wilde. For those who are looking for you—and the ghosts are not the only ones. Revealing the secrets of your past will change the direction of your future."

Mercury set his shoulders. "A future I am willing to fight for."

"Then fight you shall."

Sarah M. Eden is a USA Today best-selling author of more than eighty witty and charming historical novels, which have sold over one million copies worldwide. Her works include 2020's Foreword Reviews INDIE Awards Gold Winner for Romance, *Forget Me Not*, and 2020 Holt Medallion finalist, *Healing Hearts*. She is a three-time "Best of State" Gold Medal winner for fiction and a three-time Whitney Award winner. Combining her obsession with history and her affinity for tender love stories, Sarah loves crafting deep characters and heartfelt romances set against rich historical backdrops. She holds a bachelor's degree in research and happily spends hours perusing the reference shelves of her local library.

Find Sarah online at www.SarahMEden.com

Instagram: sarah_m_eden

Facebook: Sarah M Eden

Made in United States
Troutdale, OR
12/18/2025

44229342R00062